_£1_

YORK NOTES

General Editors: Professor A.N. Jeffares (*University of Stirling*) & Professor Suheil Bushrui (*American University of Beirut*)

Geoffrey Chaucer

THE WIFE OF BATH'S PROLOGUE AND TALE

Notes by W.G. East

MA (OXFORD) PHD (YALE)

 LONGMAN
YORK PRESS

YORK PRESS
Immeuble Esseily, Place Riad Solh, Beirut.

LONGMAN GROUP UK LIMITED
Longman House, Burnt Mill, Harlow,
Essex CM20 2JE, England
and Associated Companies throughout the world.

First published 1981
Reprinted 1988

ISBN 0-582-03348-9

Produced by Longman Group (FE) Ltd
Printed in Hong Kong

Contents

Part 1

Introduction

Life of Geoffrey Chaucer

Not very much is known of Chaucer's life. Even the exact date of his birth is unknown, but when giving evidence at a trial in 1386 Chaucer admitted to being 'forty years old and more'. We know also that by 1359 he was old enough to be a soldier, for in this year he took part in a campaign in France. A date of 1343 or 1344 for his birth is therefore a reasonable guess.

Chaucer's father, John Chaucer, was a prosperous wine-merchant, whose services were employed on several occasions by King Edward III (1327–77). Geoffrey's first employment was as a page-boy in the service of Elizabeth, Countess of Ulster, whose husband, Prince Lionel, was a son of King Edward. Chaucer held this post in 1357. In 1359–60, during the wars in France, he was taken prisoner near Reims. King Edward contributed £16, a large sum at that time, to his ransom, and must therefore have valued his services highly.

About 1366, Chaucer married Philippa de Roet. Her sister Katherine was the mistress, and later the wife, of John of Gaunt, another son of King Edward. Chaucer was thus a friend and brother-in-law of one of the most powerful men in the kingdom. One of Chaucer's early poems, *The Book of the Duchess*, was written in 1369 to commemorate the death of John of Gaunt's first wife Blanche.

From 1368 onwards Chaucer was employed several times on diplomatic missions in Europe. In 1372 he travelled to Genoa, in Italy, to negotiate a commercial contract with the Genoese. On this occasion he also visited Florence, the literary centre of Italy. This journey may have provided him with his first contact with Italian literature, which was to be a major influence on his own writing.

In the course of his life Chaucer held a number of posts in the public service, including Controller of Customs in the port of London, Member of Parliament and Clerk of the King's Works. He died on 25 October 1400, and was buried in Westminster Abbey, where his tomb may still be seen.

The official records show that Chaucer was a diplomat and a shrewd man of affairs. They never mention the fact that he was also a prolific and accomplished poet, indeed the greatest English poet of his time.

The last of his many writings, still incomplete at the time of his death, was *The Canterbury Tales*, a collection of stories of which *The Wife of Bath's Prologue and Tale* forms a part.

The Canterbury Tales

In 1170 Thomas Becket, Archbishop of Canterbury, was murdered by followers of King Henry II. He soon came to be regarded as a martyr for the Christian faith. The site of his murder in Canterbury Cathedral was considered a particularly holy place, and attracted many pilgrims. By Chaucer's day it had become the most popular place of pilgrimage in England.

The *General Prologue* to *The Canterbury Tales* tells how Chaucer spent the night at the Tabard Inn at Southwark, near London, before setting out on such a pilgrimage. Some twenty-nine other pilgrims, bound on the same journey, were also staying at the inn, and Chaucer describes them all carefully. In the morning, all set off for Canterbury, accompanied by the host of the inn. The host proposes that, to amuse one another on the journey, each pilgrim should tell two stories on the way to Canterbury, and another two on the way back to Southwark.

Chaucer thus envisaged writing a collection of about one hundred and twenty stories. Had he completed his plan, *The Canterbury Tales* would have been the longest poem in the English language. In fact, he wrote only twenty-four tales, and not all of these are complete.

Each tale is not only a story in itself, but reflects the character and opinions of its teller. Some of the narrators reveal a great deal about themselves. Certainly the Wife of Bath does so. Furthermore, one pilgrim will take up a theme discussed by another, and give his own point of view on the subject. Again, some of the pilgrims quarrel, sometimes violently, with one another. They abuse each other, and tell stories at one another's expense.

For example, the first pilgrim to tell his story is a Knight, a noble and dignified person. He tells a tale filled with high ideals and elevated philosophy. When he has finished, a drunken Miller insists on telling a story which he claims will 'quite' (balance, match) the Knight's tale. He does indeed deal with the same subject – two young men in love with the same woman – but handles it in a far less elevated way than the Knight. In telling his story he offends a Reeve (a steward or overseer), who replies with an even coarser tale at the expense of the Miller.

Similarly, the Wife of Bath is interrupted by a Friar, who is in turn rebuked by a Summoner for his interruption. When the Wife has finished, the Friar tells a tale which continues some of the themes raised by the Wife, but which is directed against the Summoner. The Summoner then replies with an attack on the Friar.

So *The Canterbury Tales* is a series of discussions and arguments. Each tale reflects the ideals, attitudes and aspirations of its teller, and contributes something to the various discussions running through the series.

The Wife of Bath

The Wife is described as follows in the *General Prologue* to *The Canterbury Tales*:

A good Wif was ther of biside Bathe,
But she was somdel deef, and that was scathe.
Of clooth-makyng she hadde swich an haunt,
She passed hem of Ypres and of Gaunt.
In al the parisshe wif ne was ther noon
That to the offrynge bifore hire sholde goon;
And if ther dide, certeyn so wrooth was she,
That she was out of alle charitee.
Hir coverchiefs ful fyne weren of ground;
I dorste swere they weyeden ten pound
That on a Sonday weren upon hir heed.
Hir hosen weren of fyn scarlet reed,
Ful streite yteyd, and shoes ful moyste and newe.
Boold was hir face, and fair, and reed of hewe.
She was a worthy womman al hir lyve:
Housbondes at chirche dore she hadde fyve,
Withouten oother compaignye in youthe, –
But therof nedeth nat to speke as nowthe.
And thries hadde she been at Jerusalem;
She hadde passed many a straunge strem;
At Rome she hadde been, and at Boloigne,
In Galice at Seint-Jame, and at Coloigne.
She koude muchel of wandrynge by the weye.
Gat-tothed was she, soothly for to seye.
Upon an amblere esily she sat,
Ywympled wel, and on hir heed an hat
As brood as is a bokeler or a targe;
A foot-mantel aboute hir hipes large,
And on hir feet a paire of spores sharpe.
In felaweshipe wel koude she laughe and carpe.
Of remedies of love she knew per chaunce,
For she koude of that art the olde daunce.

(*Translation*: There was a good Wife from near Bath, but she was a little deaf, and that was a shame. She had such skill in cloth-making that she surpassed the people of Ypres and Ghent. In all her parish there was no wife who dared to go up and make her offering before her at Mass. And if any did, the Wife would be so angry as to be out of charity. Her kerchiefs were of fine quality; I dare say that those she wore on her head on a Sunday weighed ten pounds. Her stockings were of fine red scarlet, fastened tightly, and her shoes fresh and new. Her face was bold, and fair, and ruddy coloured. She had been a worthy woman all her life. She had married five husbands in church, apart from other companions in her youth – but there's no need to go into that now. She had been three times to Jerusalem; she had passed over many a strange river. She had been to Rome, and to Boulogne, to Santiago de Compostela in Galicia, and to Cologne. She knew a lot about wandering around. To tell the truth, she had a gap between her front teeth. She sat easily upon an ambling horse, wearing a fine wimple and with a hat as big as a buckler or shield. She wore an over-skirt around her large hips, and a pair of sharp spurs on her feet. She could laugh and chatter well in company. She knew remedies for love well enough, for she knew all the tricks of that art.)

The Wife is one of the most striking characters on the pilgrimage. She is a bold, assertive personality. She dresses flamboyantly. She will not tolerate anyone attempting to claim precedence over her. She has been the death of five husbands. She has a taste for the strange, adventurous and exotic, which has taken her into curious and remote corners of the world, as well as into her five marriages.

This account of her personality is very considerably amplified by the Wife herself in the prologue to her tale. There she confesses to all the deceits and wiles charged against women in the long tradition of anti-feminist satire.

The anti-feminist tradition

From very early times men have written disparagingly about women. Writers have satirised in particular their deceitfulness, garrulousness, cruelty and lechery. There are many examples of anti-feminist writing in the Bible, in both the Old and the New Testaments and in the Apocrypha. For example, Ecclesiasticus 25 and Proverbs 7 warn against the wickedness of women. Some of St Paul's letters show a mistrust of women; see, for example, 1 Corinthians 7.

In the Christian Church there has always been a tradition which exalts virginity, and accordingly downgrades the married state and shows caution, or even hostility, towards women. A notable example is the tract of St Jerome (AD 342–420) *Against Jovinian*. Jovinian (*d.* AD

405) had denied that virginity was a higher state than marriage. Jerome maintained the opposite viewpoint.

But anti-feminist writing was not confined to Christians. Pagan writers of antiquity had also denigrated women. The Greek philosopher Theophrastus (371–287BC), a pupil of Aristotle (384–322BC), the Athenian philosopher, scientist and physician, was believed in the middle ages to be the author of *The Golden Book on Marriage*, which survives only in an excerpt quoted by Jerome in his tract against Jovinian. It is full of anti-feminist sentiment.

Latin writers also wrote in this way. They include the Roman Lucretius (99–55BC), who in his *De Rerum Natura* ('On the Nature of Things') lists the faults of women. Ovid (43BC–AD18) in his *Remedia Amoris* ('Remedies for Love'), advises one in love to call to mind the faults of his mistress, and gives a long catalogue of female follies. Chaucer's remark about the Wife, *Of remedies of love she knew per chaunce*, is a clear allusion to this work. The satirical poet Juvenal (first–second century AD) attacked the faults of women, especially in his sixth Satire.

The anti-feminist tradition flourished in the middle ages. Walter Map (1140–1209) in his *De Nugis Curialium* ('Courtier's Trifles'), a collection of more or less amusing anecdotes, includes 'The Advice of Valerius to Ruffinus the Philosopher not to Marry', from which the Wife of Bath often quotes.

One of the most popular medieval anti-feminist works was *The Romance of the Rose*. This was begun by one Guillaume de Lorris in about 1235, and finished by Jean de Meun (1240–1305). Jean de Meun's is by far the longer portion of the poem, and it is his portion which contains the anti-feminist material. *The Romance of the Rose* seems to have been one of Chaucer's favourite books, for he translated part of it into Middle English, and quotes extensively from it not only in *The Wife of Bath's Prologue and Tale*, but in many of his other works.*

The Wife's prologue

Many of the pilgrims introduce their tales with a brief prologue. Usually in these prologues, the Host will ask a character to tell a tale, and the character will agree, asking the other pilgrims to listen patiently and perhaps modestly disclaiming any skill as a story-teller. Sometimes he will briefly indicate the source of his story – the Clerk, for example, informs us that he heard his tale from the Italian poet Petrarch, while the Franklin claims that his story was composed by Breton minstrels.

*Excerpts from many of the texts referred to in this section are conveniently edited in Robert P. Miller, *Chaucer: Sources and Backgrounds* (Oxford University Press, New York, 1977), pp.397–473.

Sometimes a prologue will be more elaborate, involving a dramatic element. In the Friar's prologue, which immediately follows *The Wife of Bath's Tale*, the Friar patronisingly compliments the Wife on her display of learning, and goes on to make an attack on the character of the Summoner; the Summoner replies with a promise to tell a tale at the Friar's expense. The Host intervenes to keep the peace, and invites the Friar to tell his tale.

The Wife's prologue is more elaborate still. It is long, much longer than her actual tale (the Friar interrupts, 'This is a long preamble of a tale!') The tale itself is really an 'epilogue' to her prologue. It is a short story intended to clinch the arguments advanced at length in her prologue.

This prologue falls into two parts. The first part (lines 1–162) is a defence of the married state, and of sexual intercourse, against virginity. At line 163 the Pardoner interrupts, and invites the Wife to tell the pilgrims her *praktike*, her way of life. The rest of her prologue (lines 194–828) is accordingly the story of her life with her five husbands.

Almost every line of the first part of the prologue, as far as line 162, is a quotation from or allusion to the Bible. St Paul's first letter to the Corinthians is frequently cited (see the notes to the detailed summary of the passage for exact references). The Wife is using authoritative biblical texts to support her own views. Sometimes her use of these texts is justifiable, but often she takes them out of context and uses them in a sense quite opposite to their author's intention.

For example, at lines 99–101 she observes that not all the vessels in a lord's household are of gold; some are of wood, and are just as useful. She concludes that imperfect, lustful beings like herself are just as acceptable to God as saints. Now the image of gold and wooden vessels is taken from St Paul's second letter to Timothy, but Paul's conclusion is quite different:

> In a great house there are not only vessels of gold and silver but also of wood and earthenware, and some for noble use, some for ignoble. If anyone purifies himself from what is ignoble, then he will be a vessel for noble use, consecrated and useful to the master of the house, ready for any good work. So shun youthful passions and aim at righteousness, faith, love, and peace, along with those who call upon the Lord from a pure heart. (II Timothy 2:20–2)

The Wife reverses the point of Paul's comparison.

Sometimes her misuse of biblical texts is very comical, as when at lines 147–8 she uses St Paul's counsels on the treatment of the male sexual organ in circumcision to justify the generous use of her own female organ. Again, by the repetition at line 146 of the word *refreshed*, previously used of Solomon's enjoyment of his many wives, but now inserted into the story of the feeding of the five thousand, the Wife can abuse a biblical text to devastatingly comic effect.

In the latter part of her prologue, the Wife alludes constantly to writers of the anti-feminist tradition – St Jerome, Walter Map, 'Theophrastus', Tertullian, Jean de Meun, the Book of Proverbs. Now the Wife is herself the embodiment of all the bad things these writers had said about women. They had warned against marriage: the Wife amply justifies their forebodings. She is the creation of the anti-feminist writers, their nightmare come true. And yet she stands up to refute them. And she does so from their own lips. She rises up, as it were, from the pages of the anti-feminist writers, and quotes their own writings back at them to prove that women are the superior sex. And yet even in doing so, by a sort of irony which Chaucer loves, she provides living proof that all these writers had said was true. As the Chaucerian scholar F.N. Robinson has said, '. . . it might well be debated whether the *Prologue* is a document on the feminist or the anti-feminist side of the controversy'.

The Wife's tale

The tale is Chaucer's reworking of the popular story of the Loathly Lady. There are many other versions of this story in medieval literature. One is told by Chaucer's contemporary John Gower (1330–1408) in his *Confessio Amantis* ('The Lover's Confession'). In this and other versions, the knight is offered the choice of having the woman fair by day and foul by night, or vice-versa. Chaucer alters the tale so that the choice is between having her foul and faithful, or fair and fickle. The knight, overwhelmed by his wife's wisdom, allows her to make the choice, and she becomes both fair and faithful. Evidently she has been the victim of an enchantment, which is broken when she manages to gain the 'maistrye' over a man. The knight's submissiveness thus wins him a beautiful and faithful wife.

The tale clinches the Wife's argument that a man's true happiness lies in allowing his wife to do as she chooses. But the relevance of the tale to the Wife's situation goes further than this. She, like the hag, has been transformed from a beautiful girl into an ugly old woman. In the Wife's case, the transformation has been wrought, not by a magic spell, but by the natural process of growing old. Nevertheless she would love to be re-transformed; her prologue is full of regret for her lost youth and beauty:

> But age, allas! that al wole envenyme,
> Hath me biraft my beautee and my pith.

> Lat go, farewel! the devel go therwith!
> The flour is goon, ther is namoore to telle;
> The bren, as I best kan, now moste I selle;

(474–8)

She is, moreover, on the lookout for a sixth husband:

> Yblessed be God that I have wedded fyve!
> Welcome the sixte, whan that evere he shal.

(44–5)

No doubt she would love some lusty but submissive young knight to sweep her off her feet and to restore her youth and beauty; in her tale she does indeed speak 'after her fantasy'.

A note on the text

Chaucer wrote before the invention of printing. His works therefore circulated in manuscript form for the first hundred years of their existence. They were first printed by William Caxton in the fifteenth century.

The best modern edition of the complete works of Chaucer is by F.N. Robinson, second edition, Oxford University Press, London, 1957. *The Wife of Bath's Prologue and Tale* is conveniently edited, with an introduction, notes and glossary, by James Winny, Cambridge University Press, Cambridge, 1965.

Part 2

Summaries
of THE WIFE OF BATH'S
PROLOGUE AND TALE

A general summary

The Wife of Bath's Prologue

The Wife declares that even without the aid of 'authority' she has sufficient experience to talk of woe in marriage. She has been married five times, if so many marriages are permissible. Many biblical texts seem to authorise bigamy. The Bible nowhere insists on virginity. Only those wishing to be perfect need remain virgins, and she is not one of these. Her husband may enjoy her body as often as he wishes, but will suffer slavery and tribulation while she is his wife.

The Pardoner interrupts. He was about to marry, but now wonders if this is wise. The Wife advises him to listen to her tale before deciding. He asks her to proceed and tell the company of her practices. She agrees, asking them all not to take offence at anything she says, for she is speaking in fun.

Three of the Wife's husbands had been good, and two bad. The three good ones were rich and old, and could scarcely make love to her. It amuses her to think how hard she made them work at night. Furthermore, she used to nag them mercilessly. She would accuse them of misconduct with her neighbour's wife, and complain that they were always getting drunk and chiding her. All her accusations were quite false.

Her fourth husband had kept a lover, which annoyed the Wife greatly; but she took revenge by flirting with other men, and so making him jealous. When he died, the Wife took as her fifth husband a young scholar called Jankin. But he tormented her by continually reading aloud from a book of anti-feminist writings. At last she grew so angry that she tore three pages from his book, and knocked him into the fireplace. In return he struck her on the head so violently that she was rendered deaf. She fell down and pretended at first to be dead. This frightened Jankin so much that he promised never to strike her again, allowed her to do as she wished henceforth, and burned his book. From that day on they never quarrelled again.

And now, says the Wife, she will tell her tale, if the company will listen.

The words between the Summoner and the Friar

The Friar laughed, declaring that this was a long preamble of a tale. The Summoner told him to be quiet. An argument developed between them, and each promised to tell tales at the other's expense.

The Wife of Bath's Tale

In King Arthur's days lived a knight who raped a girl. For this offence he was condemned to death, but the queen begged for mercy on his behalf. King Arthur allowed her to do as she wished with him. She said she would spare his life if he could answer the question, 'What is it that women most desire?' She gave him a year to find the answer. For a long time he made enquiries, but could not find the right answer.

At last as he rode beside a forest, he saw a group of ladies dancing. As he approached, they vanished, leaving only a very ugly old woman. This old woman told him the answer, on condition that he would grant her the next thing she asked of him.

Armed with this answer, the knight went before the queen and told her that the thing women desire most is to exercise dominion over their husbands and lovers. All agreed that this was correct. The ugly old woman then asked the knight to marry her, and in accordance with his promise he was forced to do so.

On their wedding night the young man was very sad. His bride asked him the cause of his sorrow, and he replied that she was ugly and old and of common parentage. She explained to him at length that these qualities are not to be despised. Nobility is not conferred by birth, but by character. Age should be respected and honoured, and like ugliness, it is a great guardian of chastity.

Finally she invited him to choose whether she should be ugly but faithful, or beautiful but promiscuous. He replied that she could choose: he submitted to her wise judgement. Having obtained mastery over him, she promised to be both beautiful and faithful. Opening the curtain, the knight saw that his bride was now young and beautiful, and they lived happily ever after.

Detailed summaries

Prologue, lines 1–34

Experience, says the Wife, is sufficient basis for her to talk about the woes of married life, even if there were no authoritative texts on the subject. For since she was twelve years old, she has had five husbands.

But, she wonders, is it permissible to be married so many times? She has heard that Jesus went to only one wedding, and that this signifies that we may marry only once.

Also, she recalls how Jesus said to the Samaritan woman, 'you have had five husbands, and the man who now has you is not your husband'. Why, she asks, was the fifth man not the Samaritan's husband? How many men might she marry? The Wife knows well that God commanded us to increase and multiply. She knows too that God said her husband should leave his father and mother, and take to her; but he mentioned no permitted number of husbands.

NOTES AND GLOSSARY:

auctoritee:	authoritative writings such as the Bible or the works of the great philosophers
lordynges:	lords, gentlemen
sith:	since
that is eterne on lyve:	who lives eternally
at chirche dore:	it was customary in the middle ages to be married at the church door, not at the altar as nowadays
Cane of Galilee:	see the Bible, John 2:1–12
lines 14–23:	see the Bible, John 4
ilke:	same
axe:	ask
devyne:	guess
glosen:	interpret, comment on a text
lines 28–9:	see the Bible, Genesis 1:28
line 30:	see the Bible, Genesis 2:24
woot:	know
lete:	leave
bigamye:	having two husbands, not necessarily at the same time
octogamye:	having eight husbands
vileynye:	reproach

Prologue, lines 35–76

The Wife continues: consider the wise king Solomon; he had more than one wife. Would to God it were lawful for me to be refreshed half as often as he was! Thank God I have had five husbands! Welcome the sixth! When my husband dies I shall marry another Christian man, for then, as St Paul says, I shall be free to remarry. He says it is no sin to marry; better to marry than burn with lust. Who cares if people reproach Lamech for bigamy: I know that Abraham and Jacob were holy men, and each had several wives. Where did God ever forbid marriage, or command virginity? St Paul did not command virginity: he only advised it. If God had commanded virginity, he would have condemned marriage, and then where would virgins have come from? Paul did not dare command something which his master did not order. The prize is set up for virgins; let's see who can win it.

NOTES AND GLOSSARY:

daun:	lord, sir
Salomon:	Solomon. His reign is described in the Bible, I Kings 1–11
line 36:	according to I Kings 11:3, Solomon had seven hundred wives and three hundred concubines
leveful:	lawful
Which yifte:	what a gift
myrie fit:	merry time
so wel was hym on lyve:	such a pleasant life he led
for sothe:	truly
chaast:	chaste
in al:	at all
th'apostle:	St Paul. See the Bible, I Corinthians 7:39
line 51:	see the Bible, I Corinthians 7:28
line 52:	see the Bible, I Corinthians 7:9
Lameth:	Lamech had two wives. See the Bible, Genesis 4:19
Abraham:	see Genesis 12–25
Jacob:	see Genesis 28–35
defended:	forbade
it is no drede:	there is no doubt
lines 63–5:	see the Bible, I Corinthians 7:25
maydenhede:	virginity
dampned:	condemned
heeste:	commandment
dart:	some kind of prize; see I Corinthians 9:24

Prologue, lines 77–114

The Wife maintains that St Paul's advice to remain a virgin does not apply to everyone; she is free to marry if she wishes. I agree, she says, that virginity is superior to marriage. I do not boast of my condition. A lord in his household does not have all his dishes made of gold. Some are of wood, and are still useful. Virginity is a very perfect state, but Christ did not tell everybody to sell their goods and follow him. He spoke only to those who wished to be perfect, and, says the Wife, I am not one of those. She will put all she has into the joys of marriage.

NOTES AND GLOSSARY:

lines 77–8:	'but this text is not received by everyone, only those to whom God chooses to give it by his power.' Compare the Bible, Matthew 19:10–12
mayde:	virgin
lines 80–1:	see I Corinthians 7:7
nys:	is not (contraction of *ne ys*)
yaf me leve:	gave me permission. See I Corinthians 7:8–9
repreve:	reproach
make:	spouse
line 86:	'without being accused of bigamy'
Al:	although. See I Corinthians 7:1
line 88:	the pronoun '*he*' refers to St Paul
tow:	flax
line 90:	'you know what this proverb means'
This al and som:	to cut a long story short
line 91:	'*he*' is again St Paul
heeld:	considered
freletee:	frailty, weakness
lines 92–3:	'I call it weakness, if the man and woman are not willing to spend all their lives in chastity'
noon:	no
preferre:	is preferable to
liketh hem:	pleases them, that is, virgins
goost:	spirit
nyl:	will not (contraction of *ne wyl*). In Middle English double negatives are used to make a statement emphatically negative. They do not 'cancel out' each other
lines 99–101:	compare the Bible, II Timothy 2:20–1, and note that the Wife entirely reverses the point of St Paul's comparison
clepeth:	calls
sondry wyse:	different ways
lines 103–4:	compare the Bible, I Corinthians 7:7
as hym liketh shifte:	as he chooses to distribute them
greet:	great
eek:	also
lines 107–11:	see the Bible, Matthew 19:21
welle:	source
swich:	such
foore:	footsteps

Prologue, lines 115–62

Why, asks the Wife, were our sexual organs made, if not for pro-creation? Why else is it written that a man should pay his wife her debt? How can he pay his debt unless he uses his sexual organ? But not everyone is obliged to make use of these organs. Many saints have lived in perfect chastity. Let virgins be compared with pure wheat bread, and wives with barley-bread; and yet Jesus refreshed many men with barley-bread. I will continue in the way of life to which God has called me. I shall make free use of my sexual organ in marriage. My husband shall have it whenever he wants to pay his debt. He shall be both my debtor and my slave. I shall rule over his body; St Paul said so, and commanded our husbands to love us.

NOTES AND GLOSSARY:

conclusion:	purpose
maad:	made
generacion:	procreation
line 117:	this line has probably been miscopied by the medieval scribes. As it stands it makes little sense, but if we read *wrighte* for *wight*, we could translate 'and made by such a perfectly wise creator'. This is exactly the sense of St Jerome's *Epistola adversus Jovinianum* which is Chaucer's source at this point. The suggestion of one editor, that *wight* here means 'sexual organ', is improbable
glose:	interpret. A technical term, used of commentaries on the Bible. Compare *glosen*, line 26
wole:	will
ben:	are
office:	function
engendrure:	love-making
hir:	their
lines 129–30:	see the Bible, I Corinthians 7:3
sely:	a very general term of approval – 'happy, blessed, innocent, harmless, good, kind.' Any of these senses could apply to a man's *instrument*
holde:	bound
harneys:	equipment, tackle
cure:	care, heed
hoten:	be called
lines 145–6:	see the Bible, Mark 6:34–44 and 8:1–10. It is how-ever St John who specifies that Jesus used *barley* bread; see John 6:1–14. Note also the repetition of

	refresshed, which has been used in a quite different sense at line 38
lines 147–8:	see the Bible, I Corinthians 7:20. The Wife takes St Paul's advice out of context. He is talking about circumcision. She uses his counsels on the treatment of the sexual organs to justify her use of her own
daungerous:	stand-offish
hym list:	it pleases him to
lette:	stop, abstain
lines 156–60:	see the Bible, I Corinthians 7:4, and 7:28
the Apostel:	St Paul
line 161:	see the Bible, Ephesians 5:25
sentence:	opinion

Prologue, lines 163–93

Here the Pardoner interrupts. He was about to marry, but now it does not seem such a good idea. The Wife advises him to listen to what she has to say about tribulation in marriage before he decides. The Pardoner invites her to continue, and tell the company about her practices. She agrees, asking the pilgrims not to be offended, because she is only speaking in fun.

NOTES AND GLOSSARY:

stirte:	jumped
anon:	at once
bye:	pay for
levere:	rather
to-yeere:	this year
tonne:	barrel. The Wife is alluding to the Pardoner's drinking habits; he needs a draught of ale before he can tell his own story
maystow chese:	you may choose
thilke:	that same
to ny:	too near
mo:	more
line 180:	'whoever will not take warning from other men's experiences will himself become a warning to others'
Ptholomee, Almageste:	Ptolemy, or Claudius Ptolomaeus (*c.* AD90–168) was a great scholar of the ancient world, who lived in Alexandria. His *Almagest* was a treatise on astronomy. It does not, however, contain the saying which the Wife quotes

praktike:	practices
after my fantasye:	as I feel inclined
lines 191–2:	'do not be annoyed at what I say; my intention is only to play'

Prologue, lines 194–223

The Wife tells how three of her husbands were good, and two were bad. The three were good, and rich, and old. They were scarcely able to pay the Wife her conjugal rights. They had given all their property to the Wife, so she no longer took any trouble to please them. They were very glad when she spoke civilly to them, for she usually nagged them terribly.

NOTES AND GLOSSARY:

moote:	may
sooth:	truth
tho:	those
unnethe:	scarcely
pardee:	certainly
a-nyght:	by night
swynke:	work
line 203:	'and truly, I took no notice of their discomfort'
yeven:	given
hir tresoor:	their treasure
line 208:	'that I cared nothing for their love'
lines 210–1:	'a wise woman will constantly strive to gain love, when she hasn't any'
hoolly:	wholly
keep:	care
But:	unless
a-werke:	to work
fey:	faith
songen:	sang
weilawey:	alas
lines 217–8:	at Dunmow, in Essex, a piece of bacon was offered every year to any couple who had not quarrelled or repented of their marriage. The bacon was clearly not intended for the Wife's husbands
fet:	fetched
trowe:	believe
han:	have
fawe:	glad
spitously:	spitefully

Prologue, lines 224–56

The Wife continues; I would say, 'What are you up to, old dotard? Why is my neighbour's wife so well dressed, while I have nothing to wear? Why are you always at her house? What are you whispering to the maid? Stop your pranks, old lecher. If I visit a friend, you nag like the devil. You come home drunk and preach at me. You say it's a terrible thing to marry a poor woman, but if she's rich you say you cannot bear her pride. If she's beautiful, you say every lecher will have her'.

NOTES AND GLOSSARY:

baar me: conducted myself
bere hem wrong on honde: accuse them falsely
lines 231–4: the reference is to a popular story in which a talking bird tells a man his wife is unfaithful: 'a wise wife, if she knows what is good for her, will persuade him that the chough is mad, and get her maid to back up her story'
kaynard: fool
over al: everywhere
gooth: goes
thrifty: respectable
rowne: whisper
Benedicite: a mild oath: 'God bless us!'
gossib: close friend
with yvel preef: damn you!
meschief: misfortune
povre: poor
for costage: because of the expense
parage: parentage
seistow: you say
tormentrie: torture
malencolie: bad temper
verray knave: real scoundrel
holour: lecher
ech a: every

Prologue, lines 257–92

The Wife goes on: 'you say some folk desire us for our money, some for our beauty, and some for our accomplishments. So, according to you, nobody is safe. If a woman is ugly, you say she lusts after every man she sees. That's what you say at bedtime -- may a thunderbolt break your neck! You say that leaking houses, and smoke, and nagging wives make men leave home. You say we wives conceal our vices until we're secure, then reveal them. You say all goods are tested before being bought, except wives. You silly old scoundrel!'

NOTES AND GLOSSARY:

richesse:	wealth
outher:	either
gentillesse:	courtesy
daliaunce:	flirtation
coveiteth:	covets
chepe:	bargain with
make:	mate
lines 271–2:	'and say it is a hard thing to control something that no man would willingly keep'
his thankes:	willingly
lorel:	wretch
entendeth unto:	is aiming for
thonder-dynt:	thunderclap
levene:	lightning
welked:	withered
tobroke:	smashed
line 281:	'what's wrong with such an old man, that he should nag?'
hors:	horses (plural)
diverse stoundes:	different times
bacyns, lavours:	basins
array:	clothing
noon assay:	no trial

Prologue, lines 293–322

'You say it annoys me unless you constantly flatter me, remember my birthday, and respect my servants and family – you old liar! And because our apprentice Jankin escorts me, you're suspicious. I wouldn't have him if you died tomorrow! Why don't you give me the keys of your chest? It's my money as well as yours. You shan't have both my money and my body. Why do you spy on me? You should say, "wife, go where you like, I trust you." We don't like men checking up on us.'

NOTES AND GLOSSARY:

poure:	gaze
clepe:	call
norice:	nurse

chamberere:	chambermaid
bour:	bedroom
allyes:	relatives
crispe:	curly
squiereth:	escorts
hydestow:	do you hide
good:	property
that oon:	one of them
maugree thyne yen:	whether you like it or not (literally, 'despite your eyes')
leve:	believe
kep or charge:	notice
at oure large:	at liberty

Prologue, lines 323–78

'Blessed be the wise astronomer, Ptolemy, who said, "The wise man doesn't care who possesses the world." If you have enough, why worry what others have? You shall have my vagina often enough. Only a miser would stop someone lighting a candle from his lantern: he has no less light. If we dress gaily, you say we imperil our chastity, and back yourself up by quoting St Paul. You say I'm like a cat: if you singe her skin, she stays indoors, but if she has a fine coat, she goes out to show it off. Why spy on me? Even if Argus, with his hundred eyes, were my guardian, I should trick him. You say there are three things which trouble the earth, and nobody can endure the fourth, and you say a hateful woman is one of them. Why must you bring an innocent wife into your parables? You say that women's love is like hell, or arid ground, or wildfire. You say that a wife destroys her husband as worms destroy a tree.'

NOTES AND GLOSSARY:

rekketh:	cares
thar:	need
recche:	care
queynte:	vagina
nygard:	miser
werne:	forbid
lasse:	less
thee thar nat pleyne thee:	you need not complain
line 340:	'and yet, damn you! you must support your argument . . .'
line 341:	'the Apostle' is St Paul. See the Bible, I Timothy 2:9

perree:	jewels
rubriche:	rubric
muchel:	much
er any day be dawed: before the break of day	
goon a-caterwawed: 'go out on the tiles'	
borel:	coarse woollen coat; perhaps a euphemism
Argus:	in Greek mythology, he had a hundred eyes
warde-cors:	bodyguard
but me lest:	unless I wish
line 361:	'I could still trick him, so help me!'
lines 362–7:	see the Bible, Proverbs 30:21–3
ferthe:	fourth
leeve:	dear
line 367:	'is counted as one of these misfortunes'
line 368:	'is there no other sort of comparison?'
sely:	innocent
oon of tho:	one of them
brenneth, brent:	burns, burnt
shende:	destroy

Prologue, lines 378–430

Sirs, this is what I told my old husbands they had said when they were drunk. It was all false, but I called Jankin and my niece to witness. Even though I was the guilty one, I got in first with my accusations. I always got the better of them in the end. I would deny them my body in bed until they gave me what I wanted. I won every argument; even if my husband was as angry as a lion, he would fail to get his way.

NOTES AND GLOSSARY:

line 380:	'I sternly accused my old husbands'
pyne:	suffering, passion
pleyne:	complain
spilt:	killed
line 389:	'first come, first served'
werre:	war
ystynt:	finished
blyve:	quickly (a contraction of *by lyve*, literally 'by life')
line 392:	'of things they were never guilty of in all their lives'
lines 393–4:	'I would accuse them of having women, when they were almost too ill to stand erect'
wende:	believed
chiertee:	fondness

dighte:	was sleeping with
colour:	excuse
yeven, yive:	given
kyndely:	by nature
o:	one
avaunte me:	boast
in ech degree:	in every way
sleighte:	deceit, cunning
grucchyng:	nagging
line 407:	'in particular, they had a bad time in bed'
do hem no plesaunce:	give them no pleasure
raunson:	ransom
line 412:	'then I would let him take his pleasure'
al is for to selle:	everything has its price
wynnyng:	gain
line 417:	'and pretend I was enjoying it'
bacon:	'old meat' – the Wife is referring to her husbands
seten hem biside:	sat beside them
hir owene bord:	their own table
quitte hem:	paid them back
verray:	true
testament:	will
line 425:	'I do not owe them a word which I have not paid back'
wood:	mad

Prologue, lines 431–51

Then I would tell him how sheepish he looked, and advise him to be patient. One of us had to give in, and since men are more reasonable than women, it was right that he should do so. I would ask, 'Are you angry because you want my vagina to yourself? If I chose to sell it, I could dress well. But don't worry: it's all yours.'

NOTES AND GLOSSARY:

Goode lief:	darling
Wilkyn:	Willy
ba:	kiss
han:	have
Jobes pacience:	see the Bible, Job
bele chose:	'pretty thing' – that is, her 'queynte'

Prologue, lines 452–502

The Wife now tells of her fourth husband, who kept a mistress. At that time the Wife was young and wild, and fond of drink, which always made her ready for sex. It does her heart good to remember that she enjoyed herself in her time. But now alas her beauty has faded; she must make the best of what she has left.

It annoyed her greatly that her fourth husband had a mistress, but she paid him back for flirting with everyone. She made his life a misery. He died when she returned from her pilgrimage to Jerusalem. His grave is not elaborate; it would have been wasteful to give him an expensive funeral.

NOTES AND GLOSSARY:

ragerye:	passion
stibourn:	stubborn
pye:	magpie
ywis:	truly
Metellius:	his story is told by the Roman historian Valerius Maximus
birafte:	took away
Venus:	goddess of love
al so siker as:	as surely as
likerous:	lecherous or gluttonous. The two meanings are closely connected, as line 466 suggests
vinolent:	drunken
it remembreth me:	an impersonal construction. Translate 'I remember'
line 471:	compare the modern saying, 'It warms the cockles of my heart'
boote:	good
envenyme:	poison
pith:	vigour
ther is namoore to telle:	there's no more to be said
fonde:	try
Seint Joce:	a Breton saint rhyming with *croce*. His Latin name is Judocus
I made folk swich cheere:	I was so charming to people
line 487:	compare the modern saying 'Let him stew in his own juice'
line 492:	'when his shoe pinched him painfully' – an expression used often of marriage, deriving from St Jerome
twiste:	tortured

lith ygrave:	lies buried
roode beem:	the beam supporting the rood (crucifix) in a church
lines 497–9:	the story of the tomb of Darius is told in the medieval romances of Alexander the Great
al:	although
curyus:	intricate

Prologue, lines 503–42

Now the Wife tells of her fifth husband. He used to beat her, but was good in bed. She loved him best, because he would sometimes refuse to make love to her. Women are curious in this matter. Refuse them what they want, and they'll cry for it all day. Press it on them, and they'll run away. It's a matter of supply and demand.

The Wife's fifth husband had been a scholar at Oxford, and then lodged with her friend Alison. The Wife told Alison all her secrets, and those of her fourth husband, which often caused him great embarrassment.

NOTES AND GLOSSARY:

shrewe:	wicked
by rewe:	in order, one after the other
glose:	flatter
queynte:	quaint. But notice the *double entendre*
wayte what:	whatever
with daunger:	sparingly
oute:	bring forth, lay out
chaffare:	wares
prees:	crowd
to greet cheep:	too good a bargain
prys:	worth
scole:	school
Alisoun:	in Middle English literature, the housewife Alison and the seductive student Jankin are stock figures. See poem 73 in R.T. Davies, *Medieval English Lyrics*, Faber & Faber, London, 1963. Notice that the Wife is also called Alison – see line 804
privetee:	secrets
line 532:	'better than our parish priest, as I may prosper!' The parish priest would hear the Wife's confession, and so be well informed of her *privetee*
biwreyed:	revealed

Prologue, lines 543–84

It happened once, says the Wife, that I was walking in the fields with Jankin during Lent. I told him that if my husband died, he should marry me. I was never short of someone to marry. I told him he had enchanted me, that I had dreamt of him all night. But this was false, only a trick my mother taught me.

NOTES AND GLOSSARY:

Lente: Lent is the period of forty days before Easter, a time of fasting and sobriety, when the Wife's frolics are particularly inappropriate

leyser: leisure

seye: seen

lusty: pleasant, vigorous

vigilies: vigils, services held on the eve of religious festivals

pleyes of miracles: the religious drama of the time. See A.C. Cawley, *Everyman and Medieval Miracle Plays*, Dent, London, 1956, or Peter Happe, *English Mystery Plays*, Penguin Books, Harmondsworth, 1975, for some examples

gytes: gowns

frete hem never a deel: didn't eat them at all

wostow: do you know?

purveiance: foresight

bobance: boast

al ydo: done for

dame: probably the Wife means her mother, though some scholars think she means 'my gossyb dame Alys', or the goddess Venus, or even her own 'mother wit'

soutiltee: trick

mette: dreamt

verray: true

line 581: medieval interpreters of dreams associated blood with gold

ay: always

Prologue, lines 585–626

The Wife tells how she wept little at the funeral of her fourth husband, because she was already provided with a fifth. She spent the service admiring Jankin's legs. He was twenty, and she was forty, but still young in heart. She ascribes her character to the astrological forces prevailing at her birth. She derived her lechery from Venus, and her aggressiveness from Mars. She never showed discretion in love, but followed her appetite, having whatever men pleased her.

NOTES AND GLOSSARY:
This section contains much astrological lore, something which greatly interested Chaucer. For a full explanation, see W.C. Curry, *Chaucer and the Medieval Sciences*, 2nd. edition, Allen and Unwin, London 1960. Curry devotes a full chapter to the Wife of Bath. For a briefer treatment, see M. Hussey, A.C. Spearing and J. Winny, *An Introduction to Chaucer*, Cambridge University Press, Cambridge 1965, chapter 6.

lines 585–6:	the Wife has forgotten what she was saying. Several times in her prologue she rambles on before returning to the subject in hand; compare lines 460–80
beere:	bier
weep:	wept (past tense)
algate:	continually
sory cheere:	sad appearance
mooten:	must
make:	spouse
a-morwe:	in the morning
with:	by
yaf unto his hoold:	gave into his power
coltes tooth:	youthful sexual appetite
gat-tothed:	'gate-toothed'. Having a gap between the front teeth was believed to be a sign of lechery
seel:	birthmark. The planets were thought to cause these. Compare lines 619–20. See Curry pp.104 ff. Note also that the Wife seems to regard Venus as a saint
wel bigon:	well-off. The Wife had inherited the estates of four husbands
quoniam:	a euphemism. She means her 'queynte'
lines 609–10:	'for truly, my emotions derive from Venus and my boldness from Mars'
line 613:	when the Wife was born, the zodiac sign of Taurus was rising. This sign has a natural affinity with Venus, and accounts for the Wife's 'likerousnesse'; but the planet Mars was in this sign at the time, and this accounts for her aggressive qualities
constellacioun:	horoscope
chambre of Venus:	again, her 'queynte'

Martes mark:	birthmark conferred by Mars
al were he:	whether he was
kep:	notice, heed
liked:	pleased
degree:	social status

Prologue, lines 627–65

By the end of the month, jolly Jankin had married me, and I made over all my property to him. But I was sorry afterwards; he would not let me do as I wished. He struck me on the ear once, and deafened me, because I tore a leaf out of his book. I was as stubborn as a lioness, and a real gossip, and I would go walking from house to house. He would often preach at me about this, quoting stories of the ancient Romans, or the Bible, or old proverbs. But I took no notice of what he said; I would not submit to him.

NOTES AND GLOSSARY:

hende:	nice, pleasant, handy, slick
fee:	property
list:	desire
lyst:	ear
rente:	tore
wax:	became
jangleresse:	gossip, chatterbox
sworn:	forbidden
geestes:	stories
Symplicius Gallus:	his story is told by Valerius Maximus
open-heveded:	bare-headed
say:	saw
Another Romayn:	P. Sempronius Sophus, whose story is also told by Valerius Maximus
wityng:	knowledge
lines 650–3:	see the Apocrypha, Ecclesiasticus 25:25, 'give the water no passage; neither a wicked woman liberty to gad abroad'
lines 655–8:	a proverb. The metre and rhyme-scheme are different from the rest of the tale
salwes:	willow-twigs
falwes:	fallow ground, meadow
halwes:	shrines, pilgrimage-centres
galwes:	gallows
I sette noght an hawe:	'I didn't give a bean'
sawe:	saying

outrely:	utterly
forbere:	submit to
in no cas:	in no way

Prologue, lines 666–710

The Wife now promises to tell why she tore a leaf from her fifth husband's book, and was struck deaf. He was always reading a book full of anti-feminist writings, bound together in one volume. No scholar ever wrote any good about women, except in saints' lives. If women wrote books, they would be about the wickedness of men. Those born under Mercury (that is, scholars) are incompatible with those born under Venus (that is, beautiful women), and so scholars never praise women. When a scholar is old and impotent, he sits down and writes in his senility that women are unfaithful!

NOTES AND GLOSSARY:

desport:	amusement
cleped:	called
Valerie:	probably means *The Advice of Valerius to Ruffinus the Philosopher not to Marry*, part of the *De Nugis Curialium* of Walter Map (1140–1209), rather than to the *Facta et Dicta Memorabilia* of the Roman writer Valerius Maximus. Both sources are used extensively in the Wife's prologue, but the passage from Walter Map is drawn on particularly in the account of Jankin's book
Theofraste:	Theophrastus (371–287BC), a pupil of Aristotle. He is now best known for his *Characters*, a book of character sketches. Jankin's text was however *The Golden Book of Marriage (Liber Aureolus de Nuptiis)*, wrongly attributed to Theophrastus, and surviving only in an excerpt quoted by Jerome in his tract *Against Jovinian*. See 'Jerome', below
lough:	laughed
Jerome:	St Jerome (AD342–420) was one of the greatest scholars of the early Christian Church. His tract against the heretic Jovinian is a major document in the anti-feminist tradition. He was not in fact a cardinal
Tertulan:	Quintus Septimius Florens Tertullian (*c.* AD160–*c.*225), an early Christian writer. His treatises on Charity, Monogamy and Modesty form part of the anti-feminist tradition

Crisippus:	mentioned in St Jerome's tract *Against Jovinian*
Trotula:	a female doctor or midwife of the eleventh century AD, supposed to be the author of a treatise on feminine diseases
Helowys:	Heloise, the wife of the scholar Abelard (AD1079–1142). Abelard made her Abbress of the Convent of the Paraclete, near Nogent-sur-Seine, not far from Paris. See *The Letters of Abelard and Heloise*, translated by Betty Radice, Penguin Books, Harmondsworth, 1974. Chaucer probably knew her story from a passage in the *Romance of the Rose*, lines 8745–956, on the evils of marriage
Parables of Salomon:	the Book of Proverbs, formerly attributed to King Solomon, in the Bible. Many of the proverbs are·anti-feminist in character
Ovides Art:	the *Ars Amatoria*, or Art of Love, of the Roman poet Ovid (43BC–AD18)
bookes many on:	many a book
line 681:	'and these were all bound together in one volume'
lines 690–1:	'unless he's writing about holy saints; certainly he won't say anything good about any other woman'
line 692:	in Aesop's fable of the Lion and the Man, a sculptor is carving a statue of a man conquering a lion. A passing lion remarks that he has heard of cases where the lion has conquered the man. The Wife's point, made clearer in lines 693–6, is that there are cases where men have been wicked to women, and if women wrote books they would be about wicked men, just as, if lions painted pictures, they would show lions conquering men
mark of Adam:	those in the likeness of Adam, that is, men
lines 697–706:	for a full explanation of this astrological lore, see Curry, *Chaucer and the Medieval Sciences*, or Chapter 6 of Hussey, Spearing and Winny, *An Introduction to Chaucer*. 'The children of Mercury and of Venus' are those born under the influence of these planets. 'The children of Mercury' are apt for study, and those of Venus for riotous living. Each planet has an 'exaltation', that is, a zodiac sign in which its influence is particularly strong, and a 'desolation', a sign in which its influence is counteracted. Pisces is the exaltation of Venus, but the desolation of Mercury; conversely the influence of Venus is weak where Mercury is strong

Prologue, lines 711–87

But now let me tell you why I was beaten for a book. One night Jankin sat by the fire and read in his book about Eve, who caused the fall of mankind; about Samson and Delilah; about Hercules and Deianira, Xanthippe, Pasiphaë, Clytemnestra and many other women who caused the downfall of their husbands. Then he began to quote proverbs about wicked women. Who can imagine the anguish that was in my heart?

NOTES AND GLOSSARY:

lines 711–2:	again the Wife returns to her subject after a long digression; compare lines 480, 525, 585
sire:	master
Eva:	Eve. See the Bible, Genesis 3
boghte:	redeemed
Sampson:	Samson. See the Bible, Judges 16. The secret of Samson's great strength was his long hair. His mistress Delilah discovered his secret, had his hair cut and betrayed him to his enemies the Philistines, who blinded him
lemman:	lover, mistress
kitte:	cut
sheres:	scissors
yen:	eyes
Hercules, Dianyre:	in Greek legend, Deianira gave her husband Hercules a shirt stained with the blood of the centaur Nessus, believing that this would win back his love. Actually it poisoned him, and he burned himself alive to escape the pain
lines 727–32:	Socrates (469–399BC), Greek philosopher, suffered ill-treatment from his wife Xanthippe
stynte:	ceases
lines 733–6:	Pasiphaë, Queen of Crete, made love to a bull (hence *'hire horrible lust'*) and gave birth to the Minotaur, half man and half bull
Clitermystra:	in Greek legend Clytemnestra and her lover Aegisthus murdered her husband Agamemnon
lines 740–6:	in Greek legend Eriphyle, in return for a gold necklace, persuaded her husband Amphiaraus to take part in the expedition against Thebes, where he died
ouche:	clasp, jewelled ornament (according to Greek legend, a necklace made of the god Hephaestus and given by Cadmus to his wife Harmonia)

lines 747–56:	the stories of Livia, who poisoned her husband Drusus, son of the emperor Tiberius, in AD23, and Lucilia, who brewed a too-powerful love potion for her husband, are in the *Letter of Valerius*
lines 757–64:	the story is told in the *Letter of Valerius*, though there the husband is called Pacuvius. How Chaucer made *Latumyus* of that is unclear
dighte hire:	made love to her
lines 775–7:	from the Apocrypha, Ecclesiasticus 25:16
usynge for to chyde:	who is accustomed to nag
lines 778–9:	compare the Bible, Proverbs 21:9–10
line 781:	'they always hate what their husbands love'
lines 782–3:	from Jerome, *Against Jovinian*
but she be chaast also:	unless she is also chaste
wene:	imagine
pyne:	pain

Prologue, lines 788–828

And when I saw he would never stop reading his cursed book, I tore out three leaves and struck him on the cheek so that he fell into the fire. He jumped up like a raging lion and struck me on the head, so that I fell as if dead. He was afraid, and would have run away, but I revived and said, 'Ah, have you murdered me for my land, you false thief?' He knelt beside me and begged my forgiveness, and at last we came to an understanding. He allowed me to do whatever I wished, and burned his book. After that day we never had an argument. 'And now,' says the Wife, 'I will tell my tale, if you will hear it.'

NOTES AND GLOSSARY:

fyne:	finish
plyght:	plucked
radde:	was reading
fest:	fist
swogh:	swoon
breyde:	started, stirred
it is thyself to wyte:	you yourself are to blame
biseke:	beseech
eftsoones:	once again, a second time
muchel:	much
wreke:	avenged
line 812:	'we came to an agreement between the two of us'
line 813:	'he put the bridle completely into my hand', that is, 'he gave me complete control of our affairs'

anon right tho: 'right there and then'
maistrie, soveraynetee: supremacy, control, mastery
line 820: 'do as you like for the rest of your life'
line 821: 'Guard your reputation and respect my position in society'
debaat: argument
Ynde: India

The words between the Summoner and the Friar, lines 829–56

The Friar laughed at this, declaring that this was a long preamble for a tale. The Summoner swore and declared that Friars were always poking their noses into other people's business; he should not interrupt and disturb their enjoyment. The Friar, angered, promised to tell a tale or two at the Summoner's expense. The Summoner in return promised to tell two or three tales at the expense of the Friar. The Host silenced them both, and invited the Wife to carry on with her tale. She agreed, if the Friar would permit her. He gives his assent, and promises his attention.

NOTES AND GLOSSARY:
gale: cry out
entremette hym everemo: always stick his nose in
preambulacioun: the Summoner, who is accustomed to use long words without understanding them, has failed to understand the Friar's rather technical word 'preamble', meaning an introduction to a discourse, and thinks the Friar has made an irrelevant interruption about ambling (riding at an easy pace), perhaps confusing 'preambulation' with 'perambulation'. Hence he tells the Friar to 'amble, or trot, or be quiet, or go sit down'
lettest: hinder
bishrewe: curse
Sidyngborne: Sittingbourne, about two-thirds of the way to Canterbury

---

Tale, lines 857–81

In the days of King Arthur, this land was full of fairies. The Elf-Queen and her companions danced in the meadows. This was many hundred years ago. There are now no fairies, because of the great number of friars who go around blessing the country. Where an elf used to walk, now the friar walks, saying his prayers. Women may now go about safely, for under bushes and trees there is no evil spirit but the friar himself, and he will do them no harm except dishonour.

NOTES AND GLOSSARY:
In her opening paragraph the Wife makes fun of friars, no doubt because the Friar has interrupted her. Friars were very unpopular in Chaucer's time.

Kyng Arthour:	Arthur was a legendary king of Britain. Many stories were written about him in the middle ages
fayerye:	fairies
mede:	meadow
lymytours:	friars, who were assigned a *limit*, or territory, in which to operate
serchen:	search
lond:	land
line 868:	'as thick as specks of dust in a sunbeam'
boures:	bedrooms
burghes:	towns
line 871:	'villages, barns, stables, dairies'
undermeles:	afternoons
morwenynges:	mornings
matyns:	morning prayers
saufly:	safely
incubus:	evil spirit

Tale, lines 882–918

A knight of King Arthur's court once raped a virgin, and for this crime was condemned to death. However the queen begged for mercy on his behalf, and at last the king allowed her to do as she wished with the knight. She offered to spare him if, in a year's time, he could tell her what women desire most. Sadly, the knight set off to seek the answer.

NOTES AND GLOSSARY:

bacheler:	young knight
ryver:	hawking-ground by the river
born:	carried (by his horse)
maugree hir heed:	whether she like it or not (literally, 'despite her head' – compare *maugree thyne yen*, line 315)
rafte hire maydenhed:	took away her virginity
oppressioun:	rape
pursute:	complaint
chese:	choose
spille:	kill

in swich array:	in such a case
suretee:	assurance
nekke-boon:	neck-bone
iren:	iron – that is, the axe
leere:	learn
suffisant:	satisfactory
pace:	go away
chees:	chose
purveye:	provide

Tale, lines 919–82

The knight searched everywhere to discover what women desire most, but he could not find two people who agreed on an answer. Some said women like riches, and some said respect or merriment or fine clothes or a good time in bed, or many husbands. Some said we like to be flattered, and that is very near the truth. Some said we like to do as we wish without being criticised. Some said we like to keep secrets, but that is nonsense, as witness the tale of Midas. Ovid said that Midas had ass's ears. He told nobody of this except his wife, and made her promise to keep it secret. But she could not contain herself, and going to a marsh, told the secret to the water. If you want to hear the rest of the story, read it in Ovid.

NOTES AND GLOSSARY:

accordynge in-feere:	agreeing together
jolynesse:	merriment, sport, lust
attendance:	attention
bisynesse:	careful attention
ylymed:	entrapped
as us lest:	as we please
repreve:	accuse, criticise
nyce:	foolish, ignorant, wanton
clawe us on the galle:	pick our scabs
nel kike:	will not kick
biwreye:	betray
rake-stele:	rake-handle
line 950:	'by God, we women can conceal nothing'
Ovyde:	the Roman poet Ovid (43BC–AD18) tells the story of King Midas in his *Metamorphoses*, Book xi, lines 174ff. According to Ovid, it is Midas's barber, not his wife, who knows the secret. He whispers it into a hole, but reeds grow from the hole and by their rustling reveal the secret

vice:	defect
ful subtilly:	very carefully
disfigure:	deformity
line 961:	'she promised him she would not, even to gain the whole world'
line 965:	'but nevertheless, it seemed to her that she would die'
swal:	swelled
nedely:	necessarily
mareys:	marsh
faste by:	nearby
bitore:	bittern
bombleth:	booms
hool:	whole, healthy

Tale, lines 983–1022

This knight was riding home in despair when, passing through a forest, he saw a company of ladies dancing. But as he approached they vanished, and he saw only a very ugly old woman. She offered to tell him the answer if he promised to grant the next request she made. He agreed, and she whispered the answer into his ear.

NOTES AND GLOSSARY:

goost:	spirit
it happed hym to ryde:	he chanced to ride
under a forest syde:	along the edge of a forest
lines 990–6:	the fairy dance is a common feature in Celtic folklore
yerne:	eagerly
nyste:	did not know ('ne wyste')
bar:	bore
wight:	creature
line 1000:	'this old woman rose to meet the knight'
heer forth ne lith no wey:	this road leads nowhere
fey:	faith
paraventure:	perhaps
kan muchel thyng:	know many things
leeve:	dear
line 1006:	'I'm a dead man, unless I can say'
line 1008:	'if you could tell me, I would make it worth your while'
plight me thy trouthe:	give me your word
avante:	boast

coverchief:	kerchief
calle:	headaddress
rowned:	whispered
pistel:	message

Tale, lines 1023–72

When the knight appeared before the queen's court he declared that women most desire to have the mastery over their husbands and lovers. Nobody disagreed with him. Then up jumped the old woman and claimed, as her reward, that the knight should marry her. The knight was very reluctant, but was forced to do so.

NOTES AND GLOSSARY:

holde:	kept
hight:	promised
bode:	ordered to
as doth a best:	like a dumb animal
lige:	liege
contrairied:	contradicted
weylawey:	alas! lackaday!
grave:	buried
nacioun:	birth, rank

Tale, lines 1073–103

Perhaps you may think me negligent for not giving a detailed description of the wedding feast. The truth is that there was no wedding feast at all. He married her, but hid himself away for sorrow, because she was so ugly. At night they went to bed, but he lay tossing and turning woefully. His old wife smiled and asked why he was behaving in this way on his wedding night. He replied that he was distressed because she was ugly, and old, and of common birth.

NOTES AND GLOSSARY:

lines 1074–6:	a description of a feast was considered an essential feature of a narrative by the rhetorical teachers. Since such a description was expected, it might seem negligent to omit it
walweth:	wallows
dangerous:	stand-offish, hard to get
line 1095:	'you're carrying on like a madman'
loothly:	ugly
lough:	low

kynde:	birth, family, kindred
wynde:	twist, turn

Tale, lines 1104–76

The old woman undertook to set matters right. The knight had complained of her humble birth, but true nobility does not depend on having rich ancestors. If it did, the children of noble parents would always act nobly. But this is not so; a lord's son is often seen to act shamefully. If a man does not act nobly, he is not noble, even if he is a duke or an earl. Nobility does not come from one's ancestors, but from God alone. And so the old woman prays that, though her ancestors were common, God will give her the grace to live virtuously.

NOTES AND GLOSSARY:

if that me list:	if I wished
line 1108:	'so that you would behave very well towards me'
looke who:	whoever
pryvee and apert:	in private and in public
entendeth:	applies himself, attempts
ay:	always
taak hym for:	consider him to be
lines 1125–30:	Dante Alighieri (1265–1321), great Italian poet. The lines quoted are from his *Purgatorio*, VII, 121–3
temporel:	worldly
office:	duty, function
Kaukasous:	Caucasus
shette:	shut
thenne:	thence, away
genterye:	nobility
in his kynde:	according to its nature
pris:	esteem
nel:	will not
that deed is:	who is dead
cherl:	churl, scoundrel
renomee:	renown, fame
heigh bountee:	great goodness
lines 1163–4:	'our true nobility, then, comes through God's grace. In no way was it bequeathed to us along with our position in life'
Valerius:	Valerius Maximus
Tullius Hostilius:	one of the legendary kings of Rome, who started life as a herdsman

roos:	rose
Senek:	Lucius Annaeus Seneca (4BC–AD65), Roman philosopher and dramatist
Boece:	Anicius Manlius Severinus Boethius (AD480–524), one of the most widely read authors in the middle ages. Chaucer himself translated his *De Consolatione Philosophiae*
no drede is:	there's no doubt
al were it that:	although
weyve:	refrain from, avoid

Tale, lines 1177–1227

'And whereas you reproach me for being poor, God chose to live his life on earth in poverty. Nobody will say that Jesus chose a sinful manner of life. Happy poverty is an honourable thing; Seneca and other writers say so. I consider that anyone who is content with his poverty is rich, and anyone who wants more than he has is poor. True poverty is happy; a poor man need not fear thieves. Poverty is a blessing in disguise, a remover of cares, and teaches wisdom to those who accept it patiently. Poverty may seem wretched, but it is a possession which nobody will covet. Poverty often teaches a man to know his God and himself; it is a glass through which he may see his true friends. So, sir, do not reproach me for poverty.

'Now sir, you reproach me for age; yet honourable men say that respect should be paid to old people. And since I am ugly and old, you need not fear that I shall be unfaithful. However, I will give you a choice: have me ugly, old and faithful, true and obedient, or have me young and beautiful, and take your chance as to who may woo me. The choice is yours.'

NOTES AND GLOSSARY:

his lyf:	that is, his incarnate life as Jesus Christ, who lived in poverty
hevene kyng:	king of heaven
payd of:	content with
sherte:	shirt
line 1188:	'for he wants that which is not within his power'
ne coveiteth have:	nor desires to have anything
line 1191:	'it is in the nature of true poverty to sing' – that is, to be merry
Juvenal:	Decimus Junius Juvenalis, a Roman satirist of the first century AD. The reference is to his Satire X, 21

lines 1195–1200:	these lines paraphrase a Latin commonplace: *Paupertas est odibile bonum, sanitatis mater, curarum remocio, sapientie reparatrix, possessio sine calumpnia*
hateful good:	rendering *odibile bonum*: a blessing in disguise
line 1196:	rendering *curarum remocio*: a poor man is relieved of the worries which beset the rich
line 1197:	rendering *sapientie reparatrix*
line 1200:	rendering *possessio sine calumpnia*: nobody envies poverty
spectacle:	spectacles, eye-glass
elde:	old age
cokewold:	cuckold
also moot I thee:	as I hope to prosper
repair:	resort

Tale, lines 1228–64

The knight considered this and said at last, 'my dear wife, I leave the matter to your wise judgement. Do what seems best to you; whatever pleases you will be good enough for me'.

'Then,' she said, 'Have I gained the mastery from you, since I can do as I wish?'

'Yes, certainly' he said.

'Then kiss me,' she said, 'for our quarrel is over. I shall be both beautiful and faithful. Lift the curtain and look.'

The knight saw that she was now young and beautiful, and took her in his arms and kissed her a thousand times. She obeyed him in everything, and so they lived their lives in perfect bliss.

The Wife concludes her tale by praying, 'May Jesus send us gentle, young and lusty husbands, and the grace to outlive them. And may Jesus shorten the lives of those who will not be ruled by their wives, and may God send a plague upon all old grumpy misers!'

NOTES AND GLOSSARY:

avyseth hym:	considers
sore siketh:	sighs deeply
line 1234:	'I don't mind which'
I moote sterven wood:	I may go mad and die
to-morn:	tomorrow, in the morning
to seene:	to see
hente:	took
a-rewe:	in a row, one after the other
overbyde:	outlive

Part 3

Commentary

The purpose of *The Wife of Bath's Prologue and Tale*

It is useful to distinguish between Chaucer's purpose in writing *The Wife of Bath's Prologue and Tale* and the Wife's purpose in telling them.

Chaucer's purpose in writing the Wife's prologue and tale, as throughout *The Canterbury Tales*, is to delight his readers. He does this more fully by writing tales which are not only entertaining in themselves, but also reflect the characters and interests of the tellers. The tellers, as well as the tales, are of course the creations of Chaucer. It is often said that he creates a little world, a miniature model of the society of his time. Certainly, his group of pilgrims represents a fairly wide spectrum of fourteenth-century society. A religious pilgrimage would have provided one of the very few occasions on which such a varied group could come together.

A pilgrimage was indeed a delightful social event. The characters on Chaucer's pilgrimage are intent on enjoying themselves. The religious nature of the journey is only a secondary consideration. So the Host can tell the Clerk, who is absorbed in his meditations:

> For Goddes sake, as beth of bettre cheere!
> It is no tyme for to studien heere.
> ('For God's sake, cheer up! This is no time to study.')

The Wife of Bath does not require this admonition. She enjoys pilgrimages, and spends much of her time on them:

> And thries hadde she been at Jerusalem;
> She hadde passed many a straunge strem;
> At Rome she hadde been, and at Boloigne,
> In Galice at Seint-Jame, and at Coloigne.
> (*General Prologue*, lines 463–6)

Much of her delight in making pilgrimages derives from putting on her best clothes and being seen by men. She herself describes the spirit in which she attends religious functions:

Myn housbonde was at Londoun al that Lente;
I hadde the bettre leyser for to pleye,
And for to se, and eek for to be seye
Of lusty folk. What wiste I wher my grace
Was shapen for to be, or in what place?
Therfore I made my visitaciouns
To vigilies and to processiouns,
To prechyng eek, and to thise pilgrimages,
To pleyes of myracles, and to mariages,
And wered upon my gaye scarlet gytes.
Thise wormes, ne thise motthes, ne thise mytes,
Upon my peril, frete hem never a deel;
And wostow why? for they were used weel.

(lines 550–62)

So she goes on the pilgrimage to Canterbury dressed in the flamboyant way described in the *General Prologue*, in order to attract men. She would like to attract another husband:

Yblessed be God that I have wedded fyve!
Welcome the sixte, whan that evere he shal.

(lines 44–5)

Her prologue and tale are part of this process of self-advertisement. Their purpose, as far as the Wife is concerned, is to commend herself to her fellow-pilgrims as an attractive, vivacious and lusty woman, and so to gain her ambition of a sixth husband.

Her tale can be readily understood as expressing her personal aspirations. In it, an ugly old woman captures a lusty young knight and manages to convince him that her age and ugliness do not matter, indeed are positive advantages in a marriage. This is surely a broad hint to the lusty young bachelors on the pilgrimage. Furthermore, the hag in her tale is miraculously restored to youth and beauty, things which the Wife would dearly love to regain. The Wife is indulging in some wishful thinking!

The Wife's prologue too can be seen as an exercise in wishful thinking. One thing that must be borne in mind when reading it is that the Wife is a self-confessed liar. She lied constantly to her husbands. She admits 'al was fals' (line 382) and boasts that

. . . half so boldely kan ther no man
Swere and lyen, as a womman kan.

(lines 227–8)

The reader should therefore be wary of taking her prologue as a 'true confession' of her way of life. It would perhaps be safer to regard it as the story of how she would like to have acted, what she would like the other pilgrims to believe about her. Most people telling stories about their past deeds embellish them to their own advantage, and perhaps the Wife is doing just that.

Such a suggestion may seem absurd. The Wife is a literary creation, not a real person. She has no real past. It might therefore seem a sterile pursuit to wonder whether she 'really' did what she claims to have done.

However, Chaucer's verisimilitude is such that many scholars have been tempted to think that his characters were drawn from life. An essential feature of the technique which brings about this verisimilitude is that Chaucer endows his characters with the illusion of a real past. There are numerous suggestions in the portrayal of the Wife that the 'real' past, however illusory, is not so illusory as the past to which she confesses.

The Wife would have us believe that she possessed a brilliant and caustic wit with which she silenced her husbands; that by means of this, and by adroit use of her 'bele chose' (sexual organ) she won the 'soveraynetee' or mastery from them; and that despite the faults of her two 'bad' husbands and the shortcomings of her three 'good' ones, she has had, on the whole, a good time:

> Unto this day it dooth myn herte boote
> That I have had my world as in my tyme.

> (lines 472–3)

These claims need to be examined. The most remarkable thing about the harangues to which the Wife claims to have subjected her first three husbands is that they quote freely from the anti-feminist writers. She demonstrates a formidable amount of reading in this tradition. She is not only widely read, but she has read books which, one might think, were most uncongenial to a woman of her calibre. Where – and why – would an unlearned woman have come across such books?

Her fifth husband, Jankin, had a book:

> He hadde a book that gladly, nyght and day,
> For his desport he wolde rede alway;
> He cleped it Valerie and Theofraste,
> At which book he lough alwey ful faste.
> And eek ther was somtyme a clerk at Rome,
> A cardinal, that highte Seint Jerome,
> That made a book agayn Jovinian;
> In which book eek ther was Tertulan,
> Crisippus, Trotula and Helowys,
> That was abbesse nat fer fro Parys;

> And eek the Parables of Salomon,
> Ovides Art, and bookes many on,
> And alle thise were bounden in o volume.

(lines 669–81)

These writers of course constitute the anti-feminist tradition – Walter Map, 'Theophrastus' and so on (see the detailed summary of this passage for identification of each writer). The Wife had heard all these, *ad nauseam*, from her fifth husband. He was her *fifth* husband; and a fifth husband, however illusory, comes after the first, second, third and fourth husbands. The Wife discovered from her fifth husband how she should have treated the first four.

If this is accepted, then her past becomes rather pathetic. If the brilliant harangues were thought up after the event, then life with the first three husbands cannot have been much fun:

> The thre were goode men, and riche, and olde;
> Unnethe myghte they the statut holde
> In which they were bounden unto me.
> Ye woot wel what I meene of this, pardee!
> As help me God, I laughe when I thynke
> How pitously a-nyght I made hem swynke!

(lines 197–202)

The thought of an almost impotent old man 'swinking' on top of one all night may seem funny in retrospect, but few girls would find it very enjoyable at the time. Certainly May, the young lady in Chaucer's *Merchant's Tale*, did not:

> But God woot what that May thoughte in hir herte,
> Whan she hym saugh up sittynge in his sherte,
> In his nyght-cappe, and with his nekke lene;
> She preyseth nat his pleyyng worth a bene.

Three husbands of this sort, followed by a fourth who

> . . . was a revelour;
> That is to seyn, he hadde a paramour.

(lines 453–4)

and a fifth who, having tormented her with endless readings from the anti-feminist writers, strikes her so hard as to leave her deaf in one ear, is not everyone's idea of a blissful life. Small wonder, perhaps, that the Wife is concerned to glamorise her past.

The Wife's horoscope

People in Chaucer's time believed in the influence of the stars in human affairs. They thought that a person's 'constellation' – that is, the positions of the various stars and planets at the moment of his birth – determined his character and the course of his life.

Chaucer takes great care to describe the constellation of many of his characters. *The Knight's Tale*, the first story in *The Canterbury Tales*, is much concerned with astrological influences. The plot of *The Franklin's Tale* hinges on the manipulation of planetary forces by an astrologer. The Physician is expert in his profession, 'For he was grounded in astronomye' – he cures people by observing the position of the stars, and prescribing accordingly.

The Wife of Bath too has a horoscope. We have seen that she is the embodiment of the anti-feminist writings. From another point of view, she is the embodiment of certain planetary influences. In her prologue, she has this to say of herself:

> Gat-tothed I was, and that bicam me weel;
> I hadde the prente of seinte Venus seel.
> As help me God! I was a lusty oon,
> And faire, and riche, and yong, and wel bigon;
> And trewely, as myne housbondes tolde me,
> I hadde the beste *quoniam* myghte be.
> For certes, I am al Venerien
> In feelynge, and myn herte is Marcien.
> Venus me yaf my lust, my likerousnesse,
> And Mars yaf me my sturdy hardynesse;
> Myn ascendent was Taur, and Mars therinne.
> Allas! allas! that evere love was synne!
> I folwed ay myn inclinacioun
> By vertu of my constellacioun;
> That made me I koude noght withdrawe
> My chambre of Venus from a good felawe.
> Yet have I Martes mark upon my face,
> And also in another privee place.

(lines 603–20)

At the moment of her birth, the zodiac sign of Taurus had been 'in the ascendent' – that is, rising over the horizon. One medieval astrologer, Philippi Finella, writes that:

When Taurus is discovered in the ascendent, the woman born under that sign shall be exceedingly large of face and forehead, rather fleshy with a great number of lines or wrinkles, especially in the forehead, and florid of complexion.

This seems consistent with Chaucer's observation that 'Boold was hir face, and fair, and reed of hewe.' Finella goes on to say of the Taurus-type that:

> She shall be lightly given to affairs of the heart, having a lover for the greater part of her life . . . She shall be inconstant, changeable, speaking (or gossiping) with fluency and volubility.

This again seems consistent with the Wife's amorous behaviour and her garrulousness, as evidenced throughout her prologue. Another writer remarks that one mark of those born under Taurus is big buttocks; Chaucer observes that the Wife had 'A foot-mantel aboute hir *hipes large*' (*General Prologue*, line 472).

The planets which have chiefly influenced the Wife's temperament are Venus and Mars:

> For certes, I am al Venerien
> In feelynge, and myn herte is Marcien.
> Venus me yaf my lust, my likerousnesse,
> And Mars yaf me my sturdy hardynesse.
>
> (lines 609–12)

Venus was considered a particularly favourable planet, tending to produce beautiful and seductive women. Its influence was thought to be particularly strong in the sign of Taurus. One writer observes that Venus subjects 'are strenuously diligent in the propagation of offspring and in the perpetuation of the race'. The Wife is clearly a true daughter of Venus, for she says:

> God bad us for to wexe and multiplye;
> That gentil text kan I wel understonde.
>
> (lines 28–9)

Chaucer makes no mention, however, of how many children the Wife had actually produced.

Another writer maintains that Venus subjects 'like to wander and sojourn in strange lands in order that they may enjoy the acclaim of foreign peoples'. This is certainly true of the Wife:

> And thries hadde she been at Jerusalem;
> She hadde passed many a straunge strem;
> At Rome she hadde been, and at Boloigne,
> In Galice at Seint-Jame, and at Coloigne.
> She koude muchel of wandrynge by the weye.
>
> (lines 463–7)

The same writer notes that 'they love smart, elegant wearing apparel of white, blue, and even black materials'. This accounts for the Wife's taste in extravagant clothes, except that she prefers red ones (see *General Prologue*, line 456, *Wife's Prologue*, line 559). This is no doubt due to the influence of Mars, the red planet. The writer goes on to say that they also like 'jewelry of Phrygian workmanship made of gold, silver, and precious stones for the adornment of their bodies'. The Wife loves jewelry, and vigorously opposes her husbands' attempts to forbid it:

> Thou seyst also, that if we make us gay
> With clothyng, and with precious array,
> That it is peril of oure chastitee;
> And yet, with sorwe! thou must enforce thee,
> And seye thise wordes in the Apostles name:
> 'In habit maad with chastitee and shame
> Ye wommen shul apparaille yow,' quod he,
> 'And noght in tressed heer and gay perree,
> As perles, ne with gold, ne clothes riche.'
> After thy text, ne after thy rubriche,
> I wol nat wirche as muchel as a gnat.
>
> (lines 337–47)

The writer also says that in matters of love those born under Venus 'often exceed the measure of good form'. They are 'eager, exceedingly ardent, and glowing with passion'. This is obviously true of the Wife, who 'hadde the beste *quoniam* myghte be' (line 608).

The same astrologer claims that:

> In the marriage relations they are to a high degree volatile, capricious, and inconstant, especially when they are not maintained sumptuously and in grand style; and they are certainly more contented and happy if they are permitted as many separations and divorces as there are numbered principles of love. Their amorous actions bring it about that, while they serve themselves by deceptions and cajoleries, they are pleasing and attractive at the same time, forcing the fascinated will of the lover to surrender.

The astrologers observe that Venus subjects are fond of drink and of music. One writer says, 'they are given to games and various diversions, to laughter and joyous living, rejoicing in the companionships of friends and in eating and drinking'. Another says, 'they shall be great drinkers, musicians, players upon musical instruments, and singers'. The Wife says of herself:

> How koude I daunce to an harpe smale,
> And synge, ywis, as any nyghtyngale,
> Whan I had dronke a draughte of sweete wyn!

> Metellius, the foule cherl, the swyn,
> That with a staf birafte his wyf hir lyf,
> For she drank wyn, thogh I hadde been his wyf,
> He sholde nat han daunted me fro drynke!
>
> (lines 457–63)

The astrologers agree that Venus subjects have a well developed religious dimension. Now the Wife of Bath certainly takes a strong interest in religious observances; she is forever on pilgrimages, to Jerusalem, Santiago de Compostela or Canterbury. During one Lent (the period of forty days before Easter):

> . . . I made my visitaciouns
> To vigilies and to processiouns,
> To prechyng eek, and to thise pilgrimages,
> To pleyes of myracles, and to mariages.
>
> (lines 555–8)

However, her motive for indulging in these observances is far from religious. Rather she seeks 'for to se, and eek for to be seye/Of lusty folk' (lines 552–3). Accordingly she wears her best scarlet gowns (line 559). There is little evidence of any sincere religious devotion in the Wife. Her flamboyant behaviour is particularly inappropriate during Lent, a time of fasting, sobriety and penitence. She is capable of passing the time during her husband's funeral in admiring her lover's legs (lines 596–9). She goes to Mass regularly on Sundays, but becomes furiously angry if any other woman presumes to make an offering before her (*General Prologue*, lines 449–52). She knows large portions of the Bible by heart, but uses them in controversy to maintain quite unbiblical views. She exhibits, not religion, but a warped religiosity.

This is because the religious instinct natural to a Venus subject has been perverted by the evil influence of Mars, which was also in a dominant position at the time of the Wife's birth: 'Myn ascendent was Taur, and Mars therinne' (line 613). Mars accounts for the less pleasant features of the Wife's temperament. It is the planet which rules over war, and supplies the Wife's aggressiveness: 'Mars yaf me my sturdy hardynesse' (line 612). The astrologer Porta remarks that if Mars appears in Taurus (as it does in the Wife's horoscope), 'the native shall be most loathsome of aspect, given to jesting continually, also greedy and rapacious, rash, reckless, criminal, rejoicing in causing unhappiness'.

Several writers discuss the ill-effects of the conjunction of Mars and Venus in a woman's constellation: 'When Mars is Lord of a Woman's Ascendant, and Venus is posited in it, or Venus is Lady of it, and Mars in it . . . 'tis more than probable that she will Cucold her husband',

'Mars with Venus denote the Wife full of spirit, an ill Housewife, prodigall, and that the native is or will be an Adulterer.'

The stars were thought to determine not only character, but also physical appearance. The scientific study of physical appearance in relation to temperament and astrological influences was known as 'physiognomy'. The physiognomists thought that one born when Mars and Venus were in conjunction would have 'a body not fat to the point of being obese but, as one might say, semi-fat'. This seems a fair description of the Wife of Bath with her 'hipes large'.

The physiognomists also believed that birthmarks were caused by the position of the stars at the moment of one's birth. Thus:

> When Venus is the dominant star in a nativity, her marks are found upon the loins, testicles, thighs, or perhaps upon the neck because Taurus, the first house of Venus rules in that part; the form of these marks may be either bulbous or flat and the colour either violet or whitish. They signify nothing but a lascivious nature.

It is to such a mark that the Wife refers when she says, 'I hadde the prente of seinte Venus seel' (line 604). The position of the mark is not stated. She is more forthcoming, however, about the two birthmarks conferred on her by her other planet, Mars:

> Yet have I Martes mark upon my face,
> And also in another privee place.
>
> (lines 619–20)

When a birthmark occurred on the face, it was usually duplicated somewhere else on the body. In the case of Mars's mark, it was a large red or purple mole on the right side of the face or forehead, duplicated near the private parts.

One other feature of the Wife's appearance should be noted: she is twice said to be 'gat-tothed' (*General Prologue*, line 468, *Wife's Prologue*, line 603). She has a gap between her front teeth. This is due to the influence of Mars (Venus makes for even and beautiful teeth) and signifies that she is 'envious, irreverent, luxurious (that is, lecherous) by nature, bold, deceitful, faithless, and suspicious'.

It is therefore worth paying close attention to the many apparently trivial details Chaucer gives of the Wife's appearance. These are not casual observations, but precise allusions to medieval astrological and physiognomical lore. They are used to draw a more complete and detailed portrait of the Wife's character.*

---

*This section is greatly indebted to W.C. Curry, *Chaucer and the Medieval Sciences*, second edition, Allen and Unwin, London, 1960, pp.91ff. Curry gives full references to the various medieval authorities cited.

A 'discussion of marriage'?

Early in this century a leading Chaucerian scholar, George Lyman Kittredge, wrote an essay* which has had considerable influence on discussion of *The Wife of Bath's Tale*, and indeed of the whole *Canterbury Tales*. Kittredge suggested that *The Canterbury Tales* should be read as a kind of 'Human Comedy', with each tale not only illustrating its teller's character and opinions, but also showing the relations of the characters to one another in the progressive action of the pilgrimage. It was not sufficient, he thought, to consider the general appropriateness of each tale to its teller. We should also consider to what extent the tale is determined by the situation in which it is told – by what another pilgrim may have said or done, or by its place in a discussion already under way.

Kittredge suggested that *The Wife of Bath's Prologue* begins, as it were, a new act in the drama. The Wife maintains a view of marriage and sex quite opposed to that of the Christian Church. She denigrates virginity and chastity and, contrary to the teaching of St Paul, believes that the wife should have the 'soveraynetee' in marriage.

All this would scandalise the Clerk, the expert in moral theology. It would be particularly galling in that it was expressed in theological language, garnished with many quotations from the Bible, which was the professional preserve of the Clerk. The Wife even makes some explicit attacks on clerks:

> For trusteth wel, it is an impossible
> That any clerk wol speke good of wyves . . .

(lines 688–9)

and

> The clerk, whan he is oold, and may noght do
> Of Venus werkes worth his olde sho,
> Thanne sit he doun, and writ in his dotage
> That wommen kan nat kepe hir mariage!

(lines 707–10)

The Clerk, Kittredge believed, is determined to reply to these insulting heresies. He bides his time through the 'comic interlude' during which the Friar and Summoner tell tales at each other's expense. When his opportunity arises, however, he tells a story about Grisildis, a girl whose patience and submissiveness in the marriage relationship contrasts sharply with the Wife's boisterous bullying. *The Clerk's Tale* ends with an 'Envoy', a closing song, aimed directly at the Wife of Bath.

*George Lyman Kittredge, 'Chaucer's Discussion of Marriage' in *Modern Philology*, vol. IX (1911–12), pp.435–67.

The Merchant, picking up the last words of *The Clerk's Tale*, then tells the story of an unhappy marriage between a lecherous old man and a faithless young girl. His tale is full of savage satire against marriage (the Merchant himself is unhappily married) and, according to Kittredge, continues the 'marriage debate' begun by the Wife.

When the Merchant has finished, the Host asks the Squire to tell a tale, believing, Kittredge thought, that the pilgrims have surely had enough of marriage. *The Squire's Tale* has indeed nothing to do with marriage, but it is interrupted by the Franklin, who (according to Kittredge) tells of an ideal marriage based on sound principles, thus bringing the 'marriage debate' to a satisfactory conclusion.

Objections to the theory

Kittredge's essay has been very useful in encouraging readers to see *The Canterbury Tales* as a unity, each tale being only a part of the whole and relating to the other parts. Thanks to Kittredge, it is now usual to inquire to what extent a tale is determined by the circumstances in which it is told, to ponder its effect on the other pilgrims. It is certainly necessary to read *The Wife of Bath's Tale* with an awareness of these considerations.

There is undoubtedly some truth in the theory of a 'Discussion of Marriage'. Certainly, various aspects of the problem of 'maistrye' in marriage are discussed in the course of the four tales. It is worth while to read all four and to decide for yourself to what extent they form a unified group. It is however necessary to be aware that there are several objections to the theory.

Many things besides marriage are discussed in the four tales. It is perhaps arbitrary to isolate marriage as a theme uniting them. Neither *The Clerk's Tale* nor *The Franklin's Tale* is really *about* marriage, though the relationships of married couples are significant in both stories.

Furthermore, other tales also discuss the trials of married life. The 'Discussion of Marriage' could be enlarged to include most of the tales, in which case the idea would serve little critical purpose. Marriage is, after all, one of the most common of human activities, and it is not very remarkable that many of Chaucer's tales mention it.

Kittredge's theory depends on the belief that *The Franklin's Tale* offers an 'ideal' view of marriage. In fact, it tells of a knight who neglects his wife for a couple of years in order to pursue his hobby of jousting, and on his return forces her to keep a foolish promise to commit adultery with a young Squire. This is a curious ideal.

Chaucer never seems to have made a final decision as to the order in which his stories should appear in *The Canterbury Tales*. The four tales in question do not occur in the same order in all manuscripts of the work, and this greatly weakens Kittredge's argument. Even if we accept as definitive the order in which the four tales occur in the major printed editions, they do not form a continuous sequence. The tales of the Friar and Summoner intervene between those of the Wife of Bath and the Clerk, and that of the Squire comes between those of the Merchant and the Franklin. So if there is a 'Discussion of Marriage' it suffers much interruption. Kittredge's theory may cause us to neglect the links between the Squire's and Franklin's tales and, more important for this study, the close relationship between the tales of the Wife, the Friar, and the Summoner.

The D-group

Though Chaucer never finished *The Canterbury Tales*, and so never made a final decision on the order in which the various stories should occur, there are several sections of the work which seem more or less complete. Within these sections (usually known as groups – the A-group, B-group and so on) each tale is connected to the next by a link which makes it difficult to arrange these tales in any other order.

Thus, at the end of the *General Prologue*, it is decided that the Knight shall be the first to tell a story, and *The Knight's Tale* accordingly follows. When the Knight has finished, the Miller promises to tell a story which will 'quite the Knyghtes tale' – that is, repay it, offer something comparable with it. *The Miller's Tale*, which follows, offends the Reeve, who then tells a story highly insulting to the Miller. *The Reeve's Tale* delights the Cook, who begins another story in the same vein. So there is a strong narrative thread binding this section together into what is usually called the A-group.

Likewise there is a narrative thread uniting the prologues and tales of the Wife, Friar and Summoner, which comprise the D-group. *The Wife of Bath's Prologue* begins quite abruptly. There is nothing linking it to anything which has gone before. Kittredge is correct in observing that it begins a new act in the drama. At the end of *The Wife's Prologue*, the Friar complains that 'This is a long preamble of a tale' (line 831). The Summoner tells the Friar to mind his own business, and a quarrel ensues, with each threatening to tell a tale at the other's expense (lines 832–56). The Wife, evidently annoyed at the interruption, begins her tale with a satirical observation on friars (lines 857–81). When she has finished, the Friar compliments her rather patronisingly on her scholarship, and goes on to tell his tale of how a summoner is carried off to Hell by a fiend. The Summoner replies devastatingly with a tale about how a friar is bequeathed a fart on condition that he divide it equally among his brethren, and about the ingenious means devised for performing this division.

So there is, as with the A-group, a strong narrative thread binding this section together. Chaucer evidently intended these tales to stand together as a group. This cannot be said of the tales comprising Kittredge's 'marriage-group'. The tales of the Friar and Summoner, dismissed by Kittredge as a 'comic interlude', are closely linked to *The Wife of Bath's Prologue and Tale*. It is worth inquiring whether there is also a thematic link uniting these tales, if there is some discussion or debate carried on through the D-group and of which *The Wife of Bath's Prologue and Tale* therefore form a part.

There is in fact a sort of debate carried on through the D-group, though the subject is not marriage. The Friar, complimenting the Wife on her tale, says:

'Dame,' quod he, 'God yeve yow right good lyf!
Ye han heer touched, also moot I thee,
In scole-matere greet difficultee.'

('You have touched, as I hope to prosper, on very difficult academic matters.')

The Friar believes that *The Wife of Bath's Prologue and Tale* have been concerned with scholastic topics. And so they have. Again and again the Wife raises questions which were much discussed by medieval theologians. She asks:

. . . why that the fifthe man
Was noon housbonde to the Samaritan?
How manye myghte she have in mariage?

(lines 21–3)

The great medieval theologian St Thomas Aquinas (1225–74) had addressed himself to such questions in his *Summa Theologiae*. He asks 'whether a second marriage is permissible' (*Summa Theologiae*, Supplement, Question 63, Article 1). He devotes two sections of the work to the whole question of bigamy (Supplement, Questions 65 and 66). The Wife is in truth touching on 'scole-matere'.

She does so again when she asks:

Wher can ye seye, in any maner age,
That hye God defended mariage
By expres word? I pray yow, telleth me.
Or wher comanded he virginitee?

(lines 59–62)

These were questions frequently touched on by medieval theologians.

Again, the Wife asks:

Why sholde men elles in hir bookes sette
That man shal yelde to his wyf hire dette?
Now wherwith sholde he make his paiement,
If he ne used his sely instrument?

(lines 129–32)

The notion of sex as payment of a debt goes back ultimately to St Paul (I Corinthians 7:3) but it is also used by medieval theologians. Aquinas writes a section of the *Summa Theologiae* (Supplement, Question 64) *De debiti redditione*, 'On the payment of the debt'. He asks 'Whether the man and woman are equals in the Matrimonial Act?' (Supplement, Question 64, Article 3). Dismissing male chauvinist claims to the effect that it is better to have than to be had, Aquinas maintains on biblical grounds that men and women are equal partners in the sexual act. Had the Wife read Aquinas, she would no doubt have commented, 'That gentil text kan I wel understonde'.

Not only the Wife's subject matter, but her method, is scholastic. Her prologue begins:

Experience, though noon auctoritee
Were in this world, is right ynogh for me
To speke of wo that is in mariage . . .

(lines 1–3)

Throughout her prologue and tale, she argues on these twin bases of 'experience' and 'auctoritee' – that is, references to authoritative writings, particularly the Bible. For the first part of her prologue (up to line 162) she leans heavily on 'auctoritee'. She proves her points by reference to definitive texts in the Bible. When Aquinas considers the question 'Whether the Matrimonial Act is always a sin' (*Summa Theologiae*, Supplement, Question 42, Article 3), he maintains that it is not a sin, on the basis of I Corinthians 7:28, 'If a girl marries, she does not sin'. The Wife comes to the same conclusion, on the basis of the same text: 'He seith that to be wedded is no synne' (line 51). Aquinas (Supplement, Question 42, Article 4) maintains that sex is actually meritorious, because it fulfils the Apostle's commandment, 'The husband should pay his debt to the wife, and likewise the wife to her husband' (I Corinthians 7:3). The Wife of Bath says exactly the same:

Why sholde men elles in hir bookes sette
That man shal yelde to his wyf hire dette?

(lines 129–30)

It is curious that some modern scholars have seen so much heresy in

The Wife of Bath's Prologue and Tale, for much of her argument is identical with that of the best scholastic theologians. The Wife's turn of phrase may be more robust than that of Aquinas, *But doutelees hir sentence is al oon*. What the Wife expresses is not so much heresy as orthodoxy pushed to extreme limits. She is an example to be admired rather than imitated.

Even in the first part of her Prologue, the Wife is willing to reject the scholastic method in favour of 'experience' when the former seems to point to absurd conclusions:

> Glose whoso wole, and seye bothe up and doun,
> That they were maked for purgacioun
> Of uryne, and oure bothe thynges smale
> Were eek to knowe a femele from a male,
> And for noon oother cause, – say ye no?
> The experience woot wel it is noght so.
>
> (lines 119–24)

This rejection of 'auctoritee' in favour of 'experience' is more marked in the latter part of her prologue, after the Pardoner has invited the Wife to 'teche us yonge men of youre praktike' (line 187). In shouting down her husbands, the Wife also shouts down the 'auctoritees' which she puts into their mouths. Indeed, her prologue culminates literally in the destruction of 'auctoritee', for she makes her fifth husband burn his book (line 816).

In the Wife's tale, the hag lectures her husband in bed with recourse to all the 'auctors', but here again there is a move away from 'auctoritee' towards 'experience', as the hag appeals to accepted contemporary behaviour rather than to models from antiquity:

> Now, sire, of elde ye repreve me;
> And certes, sire, thogh noon auctoritee
> Were in no book, ye gentils of honour
> Seyn that men sholde an oold wight doon favour,
> And clepe hym fader, for youre gentillesse;
> And auctours shal I fynden, as I gesse.
>
> (lines 1207–12)

When the Wife has finished her tale, the Friar compliments her rather patronisingly on her handling of 'scole-matere'. He goes on:

> But, dame, heere as we ryde by the weye,
> Us nedeth nat to speken but of game,
> And lete auctoritees, on Goddes name,
> To prechyng and to scole eek of clergye.
>
> (D-group, lines 1274–7)

He fails however to keep 'scole-matere' out of his tale. This tale concerns a summoner who meets a Fiend from Hell. Instead of running away, the summoner asks it a series of questions commonly discussed in medieval scholastic theology:

> Han ye a figure thanne determinat
> In helle, ther ye been in youre estat?
>
> (D lines 1459–60)

and again:

> 'Why,' quod this somonour, 'ryde ye thanne or goon
> In sondry shap, and nat alwey in con?'
>
> (D lines 1469–70)

and again:

> 'Yet tel me,' quod the somonour, 'feithfully,
> Make ye yow newe bodies thus alway
> Of elementz?'
>
> (D lines 1504–6)

The answers to these questions could all be found in the *Summa Theologiae* of Thomas Aquinas. St Thomas has much to say about angels, both the good ones and the evil ones. He discusses at length whether angels have bodies, and if not whether they can assume bodies when occasion demands (*Summa Theologiae*, Part 1, Questions 50–64).

The fiend gives the summoner the same answers that he would have found in any theological textbook, but warns him:

> Thou wolt algates wite how we been shape;
> Thou shalt herafterward, my brother deere,
> Come there thee nedeth nat of me to leere.
> For thou shalt, by thyn owene experience,
> Konne in a chayer rede of this sentence
> Bet than Virgile, while he was on lyve,
> Or Dant also.
>
> (D lines 1514–20)

(You will in any case know how we are made. You will in course of time, dear brother, come to a place where you don't need to learn from me. For you will by your own experience, learn how to lecture on this subject from a professorial chair, better than Virgil while he was alive, or Dante also.)

The Summoner has no need of instruction; he will, through his own 'experience', become a Master of Demonology, as great an 'auctoritee' as the poets Virgil (70–19BC) and Dante (AD1265–1321) who, in their

Aeneid and *Divine Comedy* respectively, wrote about the torments of Hell. And so it proves, when the fiend drags the summoner off to Hell.

The Summoner gets his own back when he tells a tale at the expense of the Friar. In *The Summoner's Tale* a friar is bequeathed a fart, on condition that he divide it equally between his brethren. The Lord of the Manor is astounded at the ingenuity of the problem:

> The lord sat stille as he were in a traunce,
> And in his herte he rolled up and doun,
> 'How hadde this cherl ymaginacioun
> To shewe swich a probleme to the frere?
> Nevere erst er now herde I of swich mateere.
> I trowe the devel putte it in his mynde.
> In ars-metrike shal ther no man fynde,
> Biforn this day, of swich a question.
> Who sholde make a demonstracion
> That every man sholde have yliche his part
> As of the soun or savour of a fart?
>
> (D lines 2216–26)

(The lord sat as still as if he were in a trance, and considered in his heart, 'How did this churl have the imagination to set such a problem to the Friar? I never before heard of such a subject. I believe the Devil put it in his mind. Such a question has never before been considered by the arithmeticians. Who could make an experiment to show that every man had an equal portion of the sound and smell of a fart?')

The question has never been discussed before, so 'auctoritee' provides no guidance in this matter. But there remains 'experience'. The lord's squire suggests they solve the problem 'Be preeve which that is demonstratif'. Let a cartwheel be brought into the hall, and let each of the friars lay his nose against one of the spokes. The friar who has been set the problem, being the worthiest, may however place his nose under the hub. The churl shall then be brought in, sat upon the centre of the wheel, and made to fart. The smell and sound will permeate equally to the end of the spokes. All agree that the squire has solved the problem:

> The lord, the lady, and ech man, save the frere,
> Seyde that Jankyn spak, in this matere,
> As wel as Euclide dide or Ptholomee.
>
> (D lines 2287–9)

(They said that Jankin spoke on this subject as well as Euclid (*c.* 300BC) and Ptolemy (second century AD), the great *auctoritees* on arithmetic.)

The D-group thus offers a series of increasingly abstract academic questions. It is really a debate about debates. It begins with a question which is concrete enough, and of practical consequence: How many husbands is the Wife of Bath permitted? It ends with an impossibly abstract problem, of no practical consequence whatever. There is, conversely, an increasing impatience with 'auctoritee', and a move towards 'experience', as a means of solving the problems.

These trends are evidenced in the scholarship of Chaucer's day. There was a move away from 'auctoritee' towards 'experience'. And scholastic questions were becoming more and more abstract. The humanists of the Renaissance were to satirise the activity of the 'schoolmen' as attempts to define how many angels could dance on the point of a needle. According to Chaucer, it would seem that they were attempting to divide farts into equal parts.

Part 4

Hints for study

THE FIRST AND MOST IMPORTANT thing is that you must read *The Wife of Bath's Prologue and Tale* for yourself. Reading these notes is no substitute for reading the text. Furthermore, it is essential to read the text in Chaucer's own language, that is, in Middle English. There are various translations into modern English, and it is tempting to use one of them rather than the original text. This temptation should be resisted. It is impossible to translate poetry adequately into another language. This is particularly true when the poet relies as much as Chaucer does on ambiguities and subtle distinctions of meaning. These subtleties are lost in translation, but an examiner will be looking for a sensitivity to them in the student. Anyone attempting to write about *The Wife of Bath's Prologue and Tale* on the basis of study in translation is like someone attempting to write about a painting on the basis of examining a black-and-white photograph of it.

Chaucer's English is not as difficult as it may seem at first sight. It can be understood with a minimum of grammatical information. Rather than spending hours studying Middle English grammar, you should begin immediately to read Chaucer. Where necessary, you may compare the text with the summary given in this book. Do not worry if at first, even with the aid of the summary, there are words and phrases which you cannot understand. As you read, you will become more and more familiar with Chaucer's language, and many of your difficulties will vanish.

It may be useful to read the following notes on Chaucer's pronunciation and versification. With their aid it will be possible to read Chaucer with much greater facility.

Chaucer's pronunciation

Consonants

These were pronounced for the most part as in modern English. There were however no 'silent' letters in Chaucer's English. Thus the initial **k** was pronounced in words like *knave*, *knowen*; so was the **w** in *wreke*, *writ*, *wrong*, *wroot*, *wrothe*. Sometimes **ssh** and **cch** are written where we would now write **sh, ch**: hence *fresshe*, *refresshed*, *flessh*, *lecchour* and *recche* (modern *reck*); **gh**, as in *laughe, saugh, nyght*, was pronounced like **ch** in Scottish *loch* or German *nicht*.

Vowels

These were pronounced quite differently in Chaucer's time.

a could be either 'short' or 'long':

Short **a**, as in *at, that, kan, man, bigamye*, was pronounced as in modern English *hat*.

Long **a**, as in *tale, place, face*, was pronounced as in modern English *father*, not as in modern *name*. The length of this vowel is sometimes indicated by the presence of final **-e**, and sometimes by writing **aa**, as in *baar, estaat, debaat*.

e could be 'short', 'long open', 'long close' or 'neutral':

Short **e**, as in *weddyng, men, wel*, was pronounced as in modern English *bed*.

Long close **e** had a sound like that heard in modern *tale, paint*, or more exactly like the é in French *café*. It is found in *auctoritee, me, eek*, and usually where the modern spelling is **ee**, as in *see, keep, sheep, free* and *seke* (modern *seek*).

Long open **e** had a sound like that heard in modern *air, there*. Examples are *drede*, 'dread', *heed*, 'head' and most words where the modern spelling has **ea**.

Neutral **e** had a sound like **e** in modern *the* or **a** in modern *about*. Final **-e**, that is, **e** on the end of a word, was usually not silent but was pronounced in this way. Thus *age, lyve, chirche, dore, fyve* all had two syllables in Chaucer's pronunciation. Past participles, like *thonked, refresshed, dampned*, and plurals like *wyves, thynges*, contained neutral **e**.

i could be 'long' or 'short':

Short **i**, as in *sith, in, this*, was pronounced just as in modern English *this*.

Long **i** was pronounced as in modern English *machine*. Examples are *I, wise*.

Both the long and the short sound could also be spelt **y**: *lyve, fyve, wyves* (long); *synne, thyng, myght* (short).

o could be 'short', 'long open' or 'long close':

Short **o**, as in *of, not*, was as in modern English *of, not*.

Long open **o** was pronounced as in modern *boring*. Examples are *oon*, 'one', *hooly* 'holy'. This is usually the pronunciation when the modern word has the sound in *note, moat*.

Long close **o** was like the sound in modern *note*, but is usually found in words where the modern pronunciation is like **oo** in *doom*. Examples are *two, good, boote*.

u could be 'short' or 'long':
Short **u** was as in modern *full*, not as in modern *but*. Examples are *us, putte, lust*.
Long **u** was as in modern *rule*. It is usually spelt **ou**, as in *honour, favour*. The sound usually spelt **u** is in fact a diphthong having the sound in modern *cute, tune*. Examples are *cure, aventure*.

Diphthongs

ai: also written **ay, ei** or **ey** – was the sound heard in modern *die, sigh*. Examples are *maistrie, mayde, seith, certeyn*.
au: also written **aw** – was the sound of modern **ow** or **ou** in *how, house*. Examples are *auctoritee, daunce, daliaunce, saugh*.
oi: also written **oy** – was the sound in modern *boy*. Examples: *vois, joye*.

Versification

Chaucer uses the line most popular among later English poets, that is the *iambic pentameter* or ten-syllable line with alternating unstressed and stressed syllables:

   x   / x   /   x   / x   /   x   /
For ther as wont to walken was an elf,
   x   / x   /   x / x/   x   /
Ther walketh now the lymytour hymself

                                        (lines 873–4)

(x = unstressed, / = stressed)

It must be remembered that final **-e** was pronounced, and usually counted as an unstressed syllable:

   x / x / x   / x   /   x   /
Yet tikled I his herte, for that he   (line 395)

It does not *always* count as a syllable, however, and never does so when the next word begins with a vowel or an h:

   x   /   x / (-) x /   x   /   (-) x   /
That by the same ensample taughte he me   (line 12)

It is permissible to have an extra, unstressed syllable at the end of the line, and this is very common:

```
x / x  / x  / x  / x / x
```
That I ne sholde wedded be but ones   (line 13)

```
x  /  x  /   x  /  x  /   x  / x
```
With ech of hem, so wel was hym on lyve   (line 43)

Extra unstressed syllables also occur within the line, and frequently a less regular alternation of stressed and unstressed syllables than is indicated in the examples above. Often the line begins with a stressed, rather than an unstressed syllable. This way of beginning the line is frequent enough in all Chaucer's works, but seems particularly common in *The Wife of Bath's Prologue and Tale*, perhaps because it gives an emphatic character to the line which is natural to the Wife's forthright manner of speech:

```
/  x    x   /   x / x /   x  / x
```
Thonked be God that is eterne on lyve,
```
/   x      x   /  x /  x /   x  / x
```
Housbondes at chirche dore I have had fyve
                                                       (lines 5–6)

A similar effect is obtained by omitting the first unstressed syllable, thus giving the line a *trochaic* rather than an iambic pattern. Such lines can be very forceful, especially when the Wife emphasises the trochaic 'beat' by making almost every word a disyllable, ending in an unstressed syllable, as in this example:

```
/  x    / x    /    x   / (x) x   /  x
```
Blessynge halles, chambres, kichenes, boures,
```
/  x  /  x   / x  / x  / x
```
Citees, burghes, castels, hye toures,
```
/  x  / x   /  x  / x /x
```
Thropes, bernes, shipnes, dayeryes
                                                       (lines 869–71)

Chaucer is very free in his use of this line, and perhaps we should say no more than that he uses a line with five stressed syllables and a variable number of unstressed ones.

Chaucer is strict, however, in his choice of rhymes. In particular, he does not make words ending in -e rhyme with words without this ending. So *smale* rhymes with *tale*, but not with *wal* or *al* (compare lines 261–4). Likewise *wyn* rhymes with *swyn* (lines 459–60) and *pyne* with *fyne* (lines 786–7), but *wyn* does not rhyme with *pyne*, nor *swyn* with *fyne*. Most Middle English poets did not observe this distinction. Perhaps Chaucer's care in this respect reflects his reading of French poetry, where the same distinction is always maintained.

Preparing an examination answer

The student of *The Wife of Bath's Prologue and Tale* enjoys an advantage over students of the other *Canterbury Tales*, in that the range of possible examination questions is very limited. With other tales questions may be asked about characterisation, major themes, relation of tale to teller, and a variety of other topics. However, with *The Wife of Bath's Prologue and Tale* the only question really to be asked is, 'What do you make of the Wife of Bath?' The examiner may phrase the question differently, but he will certainly want to know how you respond to Dame Alice!

The Wife dominates her prologue and tale. Every line bears the stamp of her forceful personality. Her prologue is her life-story, a compendium of her experiences, feelings and opinions. The prologue indeed *is* the Wife, in that she is not a real person, but a literary creation. All that exists of her is to be found in the pages of *The Canterbury Tales*. Her tale is not only a summing-up of the arguments of her prologue, but a lament for her lost youth and beauty, an expression of her own wishful thinking, a piece of self-advertisement in the marriage market. A student entering an examination with a thorough knowledge of the Wife's complex personality will be well prepared.

How to begin

When you have read *The Wife of Bath's Prologue and Tale* through at least once and you are confident that you understand most of it, go through it carefully with the aid of the Summary and of the notes and glossary in your edition. Have in your mind certain 'headings' which seem to be useful – for example, ' "Experience" and "auctoritee" ', 'Bigamy', 'Virginity and Marriage', 'Astrology', 'Deceit', ' "Maistrie" ', 'Tribulation in Marriage'. Make a particular note of passages relevant to any of these headings.

Thus, the opening lines (1–5) of the prologue are relevant to the 'experience'/'auctoritee' debate; they also introduce the subject of 'wo that is in mariage'. The following lines (6–58) deal with the subject of bigamy (and indeed octogamy). At line 59 the Wife leaves the question of bigamy and defends marriage against the claims of virginity. At line 154 she broaches the subject of tribulation in marriage, hinted at in line 3.

In the margin of your notebook, write a symbol against each note, using a different symbol for each heading. Suppose you use 'E' for ' "experience" versus "auctoritee" ', 'W' for 'wo that is in mariage', 'B' for bigamy, 'V' for 'virginity versus marriage', and so forth.

The first page of your notebook might then look something like this:

lines

E, W   1–3   The Wife claims that she has sufficient 'experience' to talk about woe in marriage, even if no 'auctoritee' existed.

B   6–58   The Wife asks why bigamy should be considered unlawful, though it is not forbidden in the Bible and many holy men had more than one wife.

V   59–153   Defence of the married state. Virginity is all very well for those who wish to live perfectly, but the wife is not one of those.

W   154–62   Tribulation in marriage.

E, W   163–92   Interruption of Pardoner: 'I was aboute to wedde a wyf; allas!/What sholde I bye it on my flessh so deere?' Wife warns that she will tell a tale 'Of tribulacion in mariage,/Of which I am *expert* in al myn age.'

Copy out quotations from the text which may be useful to illustrate a point, but select ones which are short enough to commit to memory – just one or two lines, as in the examples above. When you come to prepare an essay on a particular topic, you will find all the relevant material easily by looking down your margin for the appropriate symbols.

Do not suppose however that you must use *all* the material relevant to a particular question. You will not be able to remember it all in an examination. Even if you could remember it all, you would not have time to write it all down; and even if you could write it all down, your essay would be repetitive and disorderly. It is better to have in mind half a dozen of the major points, arranged not in the order they occur in the text, but in a logical order, so that your essay has a coherent structure, with a beginning, a middle and an end.

Quoting from the text

Do not attempt to memorise large passages of poetry in order to impress the examiner with your knowledge of the text. He will not be impressed: he wishes to test your critical ability, not just your memory. Instead, quote short passages *relevant to the question you are answering*. The purpose of quoting is to justify your critical comments by reference to the text.

Suppose you were attempting to answer the question, 'Discuss the Wife of Bath's formula for the perfect marriage'. Here is how *not* to proceed:

'The Wife of Bath begins her tale with a claim to know all about marriage:

"Experience, though noon auctoritee
Were in this world, is right ynogh for me
To speke of wo that is in mariage;
For, lordynges, sith I twelve yeer was of age,
Thonked be God that is eterne on lyve,
Housbondes at chirche dore I have had fyve, –
If I so ofte myghte have ywedded bee, –
And alle were worthy men in hir degree . . ." '

Here quotation has taken the place of discussion. The candidate has merely learned a passage of the text by heart, and is displaying his knowledge without applying himself to the question. A very low mark!

Here is the beginning of another answer to the same question, with a more intelligent use of quotation:

'The Wife has strong views as to what constitutes a good marriage. These views are based not only on *auctoritee*, but on the Wife's own *experience* of five husbands, "Withouten oother compaignye in yowthe". She has experience of a wide range of men. Of her five husbands, "thre of hem were goode, and two were badde". It seems that the best marriages are not necessarily those made with husbands who are "goode men, and riche, and olde". Her favourite marriage seems to have been her fifth, though her fifth husband was "the mooste shrewe". He would beat the Wife "on every bon", but was so "fressh and gay" in bed that he could, she says, easily "wynne agayn my love anon".'

This candidate is selecting short, significant quotations to illustrate his points. In doing so he is showing just as much knowledge of the text as the other candidate, but is allowing himself more time for intelligent comment. High marks!

Answering the question

The purpose of entering an examination is to answer the questions. Those who give a reasonable answer to the questions will pass, and those who do not, will fail. Many candidates however make no attempt to answer the questions. They write essays which are really 'non-answers'. Here is a typical non-answer to the same question as before:

'The Wife begins her Prologue abruptly without any invitation from the Host as the other pilgrims have and says how experience though no authority were in the world is right enough for her to speak of woe that is in marriage for she has had five husbands but she has heard that since Christ only went to one wedding she should get married only once also Jesus spoke very sharply to the Samaritan woman beside the well and told her that she had had five husbands and the man she was living with now was not her husband . . .'

This kind of non-answer is very common. The candidate is merely giving a summary of *The Wife of Bath's Prologue and Tale*. He has not even read the question. He is very nervous and in his anxiety to write down all he knows about the work is not stopping to think. That is why he uses no punctuation, but writes one long rambling sentence. Remember: there is no need to tell the story. The examiner will know it already.

Here is another kind of non-answer, not as common as the previous one. The question again concerns the Wife of Bath's views on the perfect marriage:

'Chaucer's consummate artistry is manifested throughout *The Canterbury Tales* by his sophisticated technique of creating a microcosm within the macrocosm. The characters develop their own dimension of existence within a continuum of scintillating complexity. This existential tension is elaborated by all the technical resources at Chaucer's command, producing a radical dichotomy between subjective and objective reality. The German philosopher Heidegger has said . . .'

This candidate has not read *The Wife of Bath's Prologue and Tale* at all, and has no idea how to go about answering the question. He knows that if he were to admit this honestly, he would fail the examination. So he tries to conceal his ignorance behind a veil of long, impressive words, and references to German philosophers. He hopes the examiner will be deceived, but this is most unlikely. This non-answer would gain even fewer marks than the previous one, which at least showed some knowledge of the story.

The technical term for this kind of writing is *waffle*. Do not waffle. Express your meaning plainly in simple words.

Read the question carefully and ask yourself what the examiner really wants to know. Suppose the question were:

Does The Wife of Bath's Tale *surprise you after you have read her prologue?*

Clearly, the examiner wants to know to what extent you think the tale is continuous with the prologue. What themes and interests are to be found in both?

In answering the question, you could mention that both demonstrate that:

Wommen desiren to have sovereynetee
As wel over hir housbond as hir love.

You could also mention that both show how a happy marriage results when the Wife has gained the 'maistrie'; that in both there is a strain of wishful thinking, a regret for lost youth and beauty; that in both there is a fascination with 'auctoritee', which is however tested against 'experience'. You could also mention ways in which the tale might be thought unsuited to the character of the Wife as revealed in her prologue.

The question could be phrased in a variety of ways. Here is much the same question, expressed differently:

'The Wife's Tale *is a brilliant continuation of her argument. It illustrates and confirms her doctrine . . .'* Do you agree?

Or, quoting a scholar who takes the opposite point of view:

'Chaucer has been unable to reconcile his philosophical interests with the individuality of the story-teller, and has chosen to accept inconsistency of character in order to develop his scholarly theme.' Do you agree that The Wife of Bath's Tale *is unsuited to its teller?*

Or again, more straightforwardly:

With close reference to her prologue and tale, suggest why, in your opinion, the Wife of Bath chooses to tell the tale she does tell, and what you take to be the moral of this tale.

Some of these questions are phrased simply, others are more complex and verbose. But all are looking for much the same thing: what has the Wife's tale to do with her prologue? So, if you find that the examiner has asked a question for which you feel unprepared, don't panic. Take your time, and think what the examiner is really after. It may be that he has asked a question for which you are very well prepared, but phrased it in a way you did not expect.

Gobbets

Often in examinations portions of the text (usually referred to as 'gobbets') are set for translation and/or comment. Here is an example of a 'gobbet' question, together with a specimen answer.

Read the following passage and answer the questions below:

Now wol I speken of my fourthe housbonde.
My fourthe housbonde was a revelour;
This is to seyn, he hadde a paramour;
And I was yong and ful of ragerye,
Stibourn and strong, and joly as a pye.   5
How koude I daunce to an harpe smale,
And synge, ywis, as any nyghtyngale,
Whan I had dronke a draughte of sweete wyn!
Metellius, the foule cherl, the swyn,
That with a staf birafte his wyf hir lyf,   10
For she drank wyn, thogh I hadde been his wyf,
He sholde nat han daunted me fro drynke!
And after wyn on Venus moste I thynke,
For al so siker as cold engendreth hayl,
A likerous mouth moste han a likerous tayl.   15
In wommen vinolent is no defence, –
This knowen lecchours by experience.
   But, Lord Crist! whan that it remembreth me
Upon my yowthe, and on my jolitee,
It tikleth me aboute myn herte roote.   20
Unto this day it dooth myn herte boote
That I have had my world as in my tyme.
But age, allas! that al wole envenyme,
Hath me biraft my beautee and my pith.
Lat go, farewel! the devel go therwith!   25
The flour is goon, ther is namoore to telle;
The bren, as I best kan, now moste I selle;
But yet to be right myrie wol I fonde.
Now wol I tellen of my fourthe housbonde.

(a) *Give in good modern English the meaning of the italicised lines (13–17 and 21–24).*
(b) *What in the passage indicates that the Wife is growing old, and how does she feel about aging?*
(c) *Comment on the Wife's attitude to men, as revealed in this passage.*

SPECIMEN ANSWER:

(a) 'And after drinking wine I must think of sex, for as surely as cold weather engenders hail, a gluttonous mouth is linked with a lustful sexual organ. There is no resistance in drunken women, as lechers know by experience.'

'To this day it does my heart good that I have enjoyed myself in

my time. But alas, age, which poisons everything, has deprived me of
my beauty and my vigour.'

(b) There are several explicit indications that the Wife is aging. She
says 'I was yong' (line 4) which must mean that she is no longer so,
and thinks back 'Upon my yowthe' (line 19) as about something long
past. She complains that '. . . age, allas! . . . Hath me biraft my
beautee and my pith' (lines 23–4).

But besides these explicit indications there are some implicit suggestions that the speaker of these lines is growing old. She promises
to 'speken of my fourthe housbonde' (line 1) but after only two lines
on this subject digresses into an account of her own youth, returning
to the topic of her husband only in the last line. This habit of rambling
is characteristic of the Wife, and is an indication of her age. Many
times during her prologue she wanders from the point, and in one
place even forgets entirely what she is saying:

> But now, sire, lat me se, what shal I seyn?
> A ha! by God, I have my tale ageyn.
>
> (lines 585–6)

In this passage, as in her other digressions, her mind wanders to the
'good old days' of her youth; and this is characteristic of old people.
Her memory is selective; like many old people, she remembers the
good times rather than the bad. The announcement that her fourth
husband was a 'revelour' and kept a 'paramour' might have introduced
a description of the ill-treatment she suffered at his hands. Instead,
she turns away from her painful memories towards her joyful ones.

Her feelings about aging are mixed. There is some resentment that
age 'that all wol envenyme', 'which poisons everything', has stolen
away ('me biraft') her beauty and vigour. But more evident than
resentment is satisfaction at having led such a full life:

> Unto this day it dooth myn herte boote
> That I have had my world as in my tyme.
>
> (lines 21–2)

Age, it would seem, has pleasures of its own. It may be as much fun,
or more, to think back on one's youth than to live through it:

> . . . whan that it remembreth me
> Upon my yowthe, and on my jolitee,
> It tikleth me aboute myn herte roote.
>
> (lines 18–20)

The Wife is in any case determined that her life is not yet over. The
'flour' may be gone, but she is still keen to sell the 'bren' – presumably,

to a sixth husband. And, despite her age, she will still contrive to enjoy herself:

But yet to be right myrie wol I fonde.

(line 28)

(c) The Wife of Bath, to judge from this passage, has a hostile attitude to men. All the men she mentions are condemned. Her fourth husband is branded as a 'revelour' because he kept a 'paramour', a lover. The Wife does not consider that her own 'revelous' behaviour is culpable, or that 'sauce for the goose is sauce for the gander'.

Likewise Metellius is 'the foule cherl, the swyn'. Rather than asking whether he had a point in disapproving of his drunken wife, Dame Alice rushes in to attack him. She would have stood up to him: 'He sholde nat han daunted me fro drynke!'

She loves drink and sex above all things, but her feelings about the men who join with her in the sexual act are entirely negative; they are 'lecchours' who take advantage of a drunken woman's inability to say 'no':

In wommen vinolent is no defence –
This knowen lecchours by experience.

She is still anxious to sell her 'bren', presumably to men, and will still try to be 'right myrie'; but surely, in spite of men, at their expense, rather than in partnership with them. The Wife's sadistic and hostile attitude to men thus goes hand in hand with an inability to do without them and a thorough-going pleasure in their company – after all, to have had five husbands 'Withouten oother compaignye in youthe' suggests something more than mere hostility to men! This paradox is a curious aspect of the Wife's complex and contradictory character.

More specimen answers

Here are two more essay questions, with specimen answers. It is not intended that you should memorise these answers and serve them up in your own examination, but rather that you should use them as an example of what is acceptable and as a stimulus to your own thinking. They are not the only possible answers to the questions, nor are they necessarily the best ones, but they are answers which could be produced within the time-limits imposed by an examination.

(1) *What does the Wife of Bath have to offer?*

The phrase 'have to offer' can be understood in two ways. We may ask, 'What does the Wife possess which others desire?' or 'What must the Wife offer in order to gain what she herself desires?' The answer to both questions might be given briefly: 'the beste *quoniam* myghte be'. But let us examine each question in turn.

The Wife has much to offer, both to her husbands and to the reader. To have attracted five husbands, 'Withouten oother compaignye in youthe', a woman must have many assets. She has, obviously, her much-vaunted 'bele chose', but surely more than this. One 'quoniam' is after all much like another, and her five husbands have all seen a 'queynte or tweye'.

She is in many respects modelled on the Bible's ideal wife in Proverbs 31:10–31. This admirable lady 'seeks wool and flax, and works with willing hands'. Likewise it is said of the Wife of Bath:

Of clooth-making whe hadde swich an haunt
She passed hem of Ypres and of Gaunt.

The lady in Proverbs 'is not afraid of snow for her household, for all her household are clothed in scarlet. She makes herself coverings; her clothing is fine linen and purple'. Likewise the Wife of Bath is well provided with 'gaye scarlet gytes' and hose of 'fyn scarlet reed' and 'coverchiefs' of ten pounds in weight.

The Wife of Bath, like the ideal wife in Proverbs, 'rises while it is yet night'. Her motive is not, it is true, to provide 'food for her house-hold and tasks for her maidens'; rather,

I swoor that al my walkynge out by nyghte
Was for t'espye wenches that he dighte;
Under that colour hadde I many a myrthe.

Like the lady in Proverbs also the Wife 'girds her loins with strength and makes her arms strong', though it is to do the works of Venus, not Minerva. Again, the Wife 'perceives that her merchandise is profit-able. Her lamp does not go out at night'. Indeed, the Wife's lamp burns so brightly as to shed its beams far afield:

He is to greet a nygard that wolde werne
A man to lighte a candle at his lanterne;
He shal have never the lasse light, pardee.

Dame Alice is capable of being an excellent wife to any man, provided that he will obey her rules:

. . . I was to hym as kynde
As any wyf from Denmark unto Ynde,
And also trewe . . .

The rules however are very strict. You must allow her 'al the soveraynetee', and be prepared to say 'Do as thee lust the terme of al thy lyf'. You must give her the keys of your money-box, and allow her liberty to do as she likes with herself and your money:

> Thou sholdest seye, 'Wyf, go wher thee liste;
> Taak youre disport, I wol nat leve no talys.
> I know yow for a trewe wyf, dame Alys'.

If you want to live happily with the Wife of Bath, you must forswear jealousy. Like the knight in her tale, you must be prepared to

> . . . take youre aventure of the repair
> That shal be to youre hous by cause of me,
> Or in som oother place, may wel be.

This is after all not an unreasonable condition:

> Have thou ynogh, what thar thee recche or care
> How myrily that othere folkes fare?

And, if you will but give her the liberty to do otherwise, she may well keep her 'bele chose' 'for youre owene tooth'.

So the Wife of Bath has plenty to offer to a sixth husband. Life with her would sometimes be painful:

> O Lord! the peyne I dide hem and the wo.

It would frequently be exhausting:

> As help me God, I laughe whan I thynke
> How pitously a-nyght I made hem swynke!

But it would never be boring.

To the present-day reader also the Wife has much to offer. We cannot now test her claims for her 'bele chose', 'By preeve which that is demonstratif', but neither need we fear her tongue, her extravagance, her deceit, her cruelty. We may simply enjoy, from a safe distance, her wit, energy and shamelessness. As with so many of Chaucer's characters, it is her unashamed delight in being herself that makes her so attractive. Her prologue may be a confession, but it is no apology.

An adjective Chaucer frequently uses of his characters is *worthy*. But worth, for Chaucer, has little to do with moral excellence or social rank or wealth or learning. Simply to be human, and to be a remarkable example of humanity, is to be worthy. One may be a worthy scoundrel. Thus the Friar is 'this worthy lymytour', the Merchant is 'this worthy man', and the Franklin is 'a worthy vavasour'. In this sense the Wife is certainly worthy, and Chaucer says of her:

> She was a worthy womman al hir lyve.

But he goes on immediately:

> Housbondes at chirche dore she hadde fyve.

It is the sheer quantity of her wifeliness that makes her so worthy. She is the archetypal Wife, the Archwife.

If we consider what the Wife *has* to offer in order to gain what she desires, a sadder picture emerges. There is no doubt what she desires – a sixth husband:

> Welcome the sixte, whan that evere he shal.

She is perfectly frank about this:

> An housbonde I wol have, I wol nat lette.

Her tale maintains that one should not hesitate to marry a woman because she is old, and ugly, and common. This is a broad hint to her fellow-pilgrims.

And therein lies the sadness. The Wife has not so much to offer as formerly:

> The flour is goon, ther is namoore to telle;
> The bren, as I best kan, now moste I selle.

Her face is now 'boold' and 'reed of hewe'; she has 'hipes large'. Benjamin Franklin always maintained that a woman's decay begins at her extremities and works inwards, so perhaps the Wife still has 'the beste *quoniam* myghte be'. If so, it is her last remaining physical asset, and no wonder she hawks it around so single-mindedly:

> In wyfhod I wol use myn instrument
> As frely as my Makere hath it sent.
> If I be daungerous, God yeve me sorwe!
> Myn housbonde shal it have bothe eve and morwe,
> Whan that hym list come forth and paye his dette.

---

(2) *'Her choice of a fairy-tale is at best improbable.' Is* The Wife of Bath's Tale *really suited to its teller?*

It is hard to see why the choice of a fairy-tale would be improbable for the Wife of Bath. The supposition behind the suggestion is that such stories were the preserve of a higher stratum of society than that to which the Wife of Bath belongs. But by the fourteenth century, stories of elf-queens and fairies, especially if set in the court of King Arthur, were very popular.

For example, Thomas Chestre's *Sir Launfal*, which was certainly not intended for a courtly audience, tells of a knight of Arthur's court who falls in love with a fairy woman who rescues him from the wrath of Queen Guinevere. The subject matter is not very different from that of

The Wife of Bath's Tale. Again, Chaucer's own *Tale of Sir Thopas*, his parody of popular Middle English romances, concerns a knight who rides off in quest of an elf-queen. So a tale set 'In th'olde dayes of the Kyng Arthour' about 'The elf-queene, with hir joly compaignye' would be exactly the kind of literature with which the Wife of Bath would be familiar.

An analysis of her tale reveals little or nothing which is not suited to the Wife. It begins with the mention of fairies and digresses almost immediately into a satirical attack on friars. The Wife's habit of digression is well attested in her prologue, and the anti-fraternal nature of this digression arises out of the Friar's previous interruption. So these lines are well suited to their teller.

The first thing that happens in the tale is a rape. A story that begins with a rape and ends with a man and woman making love in bed is pretty well aligned with the Wife's own interests. And the situation in which a woman – the Queen – has a man in her power, 'To chese wheither she wolde hym save or spille', in which she has indeed 'al the soveraynetee' over him, is surely close to the Wife's heart.

The Queen sends a knight on a quest to discover what it is that women most desire. The answer turns out to be:

Wommen desiren to have sovereynetee
As wel over hir housbond as hir love,
And for to been in maistrie hym above.

This is the Wife of Bath's own opinion, an opinion stated forcibly enough in her prologue. It is arrived at by way of a long discussion of the things women desire most. Such a discussion comes very aptly from the lips of the Wife, and it is during this passage that her own voice may be heard most clearly:

Somme seyde that oure hertes been moost esed
Whan that we been yflatered and yplesed.
He gooth ful ny the sothe, I wol nat lye.
A man shal wynne us best with flaterye.

The discussion digresses into a retelling of Ovid's tale of King Midas, which has little to do with the knight's situation but has much to say about the Wife's garrulity. She too is unable to keep her husband's most intimate secrets:

For hadde myn housbonde pissed on a wal,
Or doon a thyng that sholde han cost his lyf,
To hire, and to another worthy wyf,
And to my nece, which that I loved weel,
I wolde han toold his conseil every deel.

It is notable that the Wife changes Ovid's story, making it Midas's wife, not his barber, who betrays his secret. This change relates the digression more closely to the Wife's own situation. Notice, too, how abruptly she breaks off the digression to return to the main thread of her story:

> The remenant of the tale if ye wol heere,
> Redeth Ovyde, and ther ye may it leere.
> This knyght, of which my tale is specially . . .

This habit of rambling on and then pulling up sharply could be amply illustrated from the Wife's prologue.

The ugly old hag of the tale gains herself a lusty young husband through her wisdom. This clearly reflects the Wife's own wishes. She is now ugly:

> But age, allas! that al wol envenyme,
> Hath me biraft my beautee and my pith.

And she would dearly love to gain a sixth husband:

> Welcome the sixte, whan that evere he shal.

In her curtain-lecture the hag convinces her husband that age and ugliness are no bar to a happy marriage. This seems to be a hint to the Wife's bachelor companions on the pilgrimage. Furthermore the hag wins the 'maistrie' from her husband, just as the Wife had won 'By maistrie, al the soveraynetee'. The parallel with the Wife's own situation is close, and lest anyone should overlook it she concludes:

> . . . Jhesu Crist us sende
> Housbondes meeke, yonge, and fresshe abedde.

The lecture to which the hag subjects her reluctant bridegroom might be thought unsuited to the Wife. The discussion of 'gentil' behaviour, the citations of ancient philosophers, might be thought to emanate from Chaucer himself rather than from the Wife of Bath, and therefore to constitute a breach of dramatic propriety.

To some extent of course there is a deliberate and comic breach of dramatic propriety. To have a hag from King Arthur's day quoting the poet Dante (AD1265–1321) is an impossibility. The Wife of Bath delights in dramatic impropriety, as in every other kind of impropriety. She is capable of popping up in *The Merchant's Tale*:

> The Wyf of Bathe, if ye han understonde,
> Of mariage, which we have no honde,
> Declared hath ful wel in litel space.

The philosophy of the curtain-lecture is however not beyond the capabilities of the Wife of Bath. In her prologue she demonstrated a formidable amount of reading, much of it derived from her fifth husband's book. She had been lectured incessantly by Jankin; in subjecting the arrogant young knight of her tale to such a lecture she is, in a way, getting her own back. The balance of 'experience' and 'auctoritee' in the lecture also is exactly what is found in the prologue.

But the closest connection between the tale and the Wife herself lies in the result of the curtain-lecture. The hag is transformed, restored to youth and beauty. This is just what the Wife herself longs for. In the seventeenth century Richard Braithwait remarked of the Wife, 'no doubt it would highly content her to have a taste of Aeson's herb, and so become young again'. The tale is a piece of wish-fulfilment. At every point it touches on the Wife's own situation, her concerns and aspirations. It is admirably suited to its teller.

Part 5

Suggestions for further reading

The text

WINNY, JAMES (ED.): *The Wife of Bath's Prologue and Tale,* Cambridge University Press, Cambridge, 1965. A useful edition with abundant notes and a full glossary.

Chaucer's other works

The best way to gain a deeper understanding of the Wife of Bath is to read widely among Chaucer's other works. It is especially helpful to read the rest of *The Canterbury Tales.*

ROBINSON, F.N. (ED.): *The Works of Geoffrey Chaucer,* second edition, Oxford University Press, London, 1957. The best edition.

CAWLEY, A.C. (ED.): *Chaucer: The Canterbury Tales,* Dent (Everyman's Library), London, 1958. A less expensive edition, and very useful for the beginner. It reprints the text from Robinson's edition, without the learned notes but with translations of difficult words and phrases on the same page as the original. This makes it a very easy text for rapid reading, though the book does not provide the information necessary for detailed study.

Scholarship and criticism

CURRY, W.C.: *Chaucer and the Mediaeval Sciences,* second edition, Allen and Unwin, London, 1960. Invaluable for the light it sheds on the astronomy, physiognomy and metoposcopy of the text.

DONALDSON, E.T.: *Speaking of Chaucer,* Athlone Press, London, 1970. A very good book on Chaucer; only a few references to *The Wife of Bath's Prologue and Tale.*

HUSSEY, M., SPEARING, A.C. AND WINNY, J.: *An Introduction to Chaucer,* Cambridge University Press, Cambridge, 1965. A useful basic introduction.

MILLER, ROBERT P.: *Chaucer: Sources and Backgrounds,* Oxford University Press, New York, 1977. Invaluable for the study of Chaucer's sources. Particularly relevant to *The Wife of Bath's Prologue and Tale* is Chapter 8, 'The Antifeminist Tradition', pp.397–473.

WAGENKNECHT, EDWARD: *Chaucer: Modern Essays in Criticism,* Oxford University Press, New York, 1959. Reprints three articles which are useful in studying the Wife of Bath:
(1) W.C. Curry, 'The Wife of Bath' (from *Chaucer and the Mediaeval Sciences*), pp.166–87.
(2) G.L. Kittredge, 'Chaucer's Discussion of Marriage' (from *Modern Philology*, ix [1911–12], 435–67), pp. 188–215.
(3) H.B. Hinckley, 'The Debate on Marriage in *The Canterbury Tales*' (from *Publications of the Modern Language Association of America*, xxxii [1917], 292–305), pp.216–25.

The author of these notes

W.G. EAST was educated at Keble College, Oxford, and Yale University. His doctoral research was on the twelfth-century historical novelist Geoffrey of Monmouth. He has taught Middle English in the National University of Ireland and at the Centre for Medieval and Renaissance Studies at Oxford.

He is now in Holy Orders, but continues to publish in various areas of medieval literature, including Chaucer and Geoffrey of Monmouth. He has written a study of *The Franklin's Tale* in the York Notes series.